B

Jack Russelled to Death

Cavaliered to Death

Bichoned to Death

Shepherded to Death

Doodled to Death

Corgied to Death

Aussied to Death

Dachshund to Death

Labradored to Death

Puppied to Death

LABRADORED TO DEATH

CB WILSON

For Rebecca Witters
You are the friend everyone wishes they had

CONTENTS

PRAISE FOR BARKVIEW MYSTERIES

See what readers are saying about Barkview Mysteries in these five-star reviews:

"If you are looking for a mystery to tax your clue-connecting skills then Doodled to Death is one novel you should read. Its quirky humor and intelligent banter give it the feel of a Nancy Drew and Miss Marple murder mysteries hybrid with an even more exciting conclusion."
—Reader's Favorite, 5-star review

"I couldn't put the book down! The writing is top-caliber, the characterization three-dimensional, the concept clever, and the plot is compelling. (Not to mention the cute, opinionated dogs...) This cozy mystery will enthrall both dog lovers and history lovers."
—Lori H, Amazon

"CB Wilson is a fun, fresh voice on the cozy mystery scene."
—Sherri I., Amazon

"C. B. Wilson has done it again. Her cozy mysteries are full of charisma, they are entertaining, full of life, and very descriptive! Every one I read captivates me until the very last page. Love these books!!"
—babygirl, Amazon

"Fast-paced, well-written and clever mystery that will tickle the fancy of dog lovers and non-dog lovers alike."
—BH, Amazon

"A cozy mystery that's enjoyable and entertaining yet has the suspense and mystery that keeps you engaged and turning the pages."
—Buzymomof2, Amazon

"Another enrapturing, delightful canine escapade!!!"
—Uma V., Amazon

"A fantastic read for dog and cat lovers alike."
—Ex-Libris, Amazon

Wow!!! C B Wilson knows how to write a cozy mystery! So creative and definitely kept me guessing!
—DKaler, Amazon

This series just keeps getting better and this is my favorite thus far. As a fellow cat lover, I find myself going to the dark side more and more with each book. I wholeheartedly recommend visiting Barkview soon and putting this immensely entertaining cozy animal series at the top of your TBR list.
—catmom17, Amazon

Dolphin Training Center

Fishtails Seaside Cafe

DOG PATH

1. Bow Wow Boutique
2. Posh Puppies
3. Bichon Bisquets
4. Beg-als Shoppe
5. Muttropolis
6. Woofing Best Coffe

7. Urban Pup
8. Snooty Pooch
9. Fluff & Buff
10. Fiesta Chihuahua

11. Bank
12. Gem's Palace
13. Blooming Tails
14. Taj Ma Hound

Sandy's House

Homes

Oldman home
(circa 1900-1925)

Red Door Speakeasy
(circa 1920-1925

K9 Fine Wine Bar

Sea Dog Scuba Shop

Hounds Hardware

Graveyard & Ghost

Frosty Pup

Chateau Chien

Canine Christmas Shop

Canine Caramel

Salty Dog Seafood

Doodle Pad

Mutt Hutt

Dogwoo

Smy

15. Hot Dog Stand
16. Bone Garden Salad
17. Attorney
18. Escrow
19. Hair Salon

KDOG Studio

Gingerbread DogHouse
Baking Tent

Kanine

Dolce

Ciao Bella

Dog House

A Lifeguard Tower

Bark Rock

A

B Old Barkview Inn

WOOF

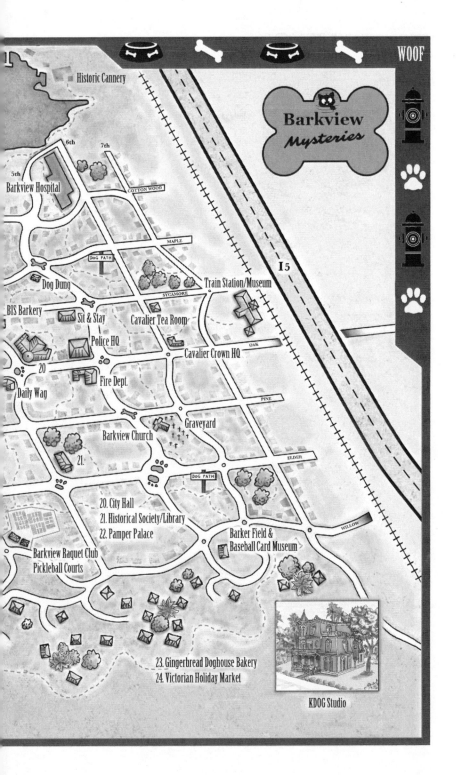

WOOF

Historic Cannery

Barkview
Mysteries

I 5

6th
7th
5th
Barkview Hospital
COTTON WOOD
MAPLE
DOG PATH
SYCAMORE
Dog Dung
BIS Barkery
Sit & Stay
Cavalier Tea Room
Police HQ
20
Fire Dept.
Daily Wag
Train Station/Museum
Cavalier Crown HQ
OAK
PINE
Barkview Church
Graveyard
ELDER
21.
DOG PATH

20. City Hall
21. Historical Society/Library
22. Pamper Palace

Barker Field &
Baseball Card Museum
WILLOW

Barkview Raquet Club
Pickleball Courts

23. Gingerbread Doghouse Bakery
24. Victorian Holiday Market

KDOG Studio

CHARACTERS, HUMAN

Barklay, Charlotte (Aunt Char): Mayor of Barkview, dog psychiatrist on *Throw Him a Bone*. Renny, a champion Cavalier King Charles Spaniel, is her dog.

Bruns, Austin: Texas baseball memorabilia collector. Related to Bertie Wallace.

Daniels, Owen: 1950s Fab Five 1st baseman. Deceased.

Hawl, Russ: Cat's husband. FBI consultant. Owns Blue Diamond Security.

Hawl-Wright, Catalina "Cat": Vice-President at KDOG. A cat person living in Barkview.

Manley, Amanda: Director of Barkview's baseball card museum. Stallone, a Basset Hound, is her dog.

Moore, Jennifer: General Manager at KDOG. Cinnamon & Nutmeg, two Cavalier King Charles Spaniels, are her dogs.

O'Donnell, Michael: Champ's trainer and handler. Champ, a black Labrador Retriever, is his dog.

Oldeman, Will: Elevator operator at the Old Barkview Inn.

Richards, Richie: Barkview Police Officer.

Richards, Hunter: Richie's cousin. He is a baseball memorabilia dealer.

Ruff, Rufus: A local baseball memorabilia dealer.

Schmidt, Gregory (Uncle G): Barkview's police chief. Max and Maxine, silver-point German Shepherds, are his dogs.

Sugarland, Carmella (Ella): Owner of the Candy Crusher baseball card.

Sugarland, Clark: Current president of Canine Caramel. The Candy Catcher's grandson.

Sugarland, Henry: Ella's father. Clark's brother. Deceased.

Sugarland, Kandy (Grandma K): The Candy Catcher's sister. Nana Dolce was her mother. Deceased.

Sugarland, Karl Jr.: The Candy Catcher. 1950s Fab Five Catcher. Owned Canine Caramel in the 1950s-2000.

Sugarland, Nana Dolce: The Candy Catcher's mother. She owned Canine Caramel 1925-1950.

Sugarland-Russo, Keke: Ella's mother.

Sullivan, Joe (Sully): 1950s Fab Five short stop. Deceased.

Turner, Gabby: Owner of Daily Wag coffee shop. Sal, a Saluki, is her dog.

Wallace, Bertie: 1950s Fab Five 2nd baseman. Deceased.

Wilcox, Artie: 1950s Fab Five 3rd baseman. Deceased.

Witman, Mel: Owns BIS Barkery with her sister Nell.

Witman, Nell: Owns Sit and Stay Café. Mel is her sister. Blur, a black Labrador Retriever, is her dog.

Woofman, Danny (Woof): Owns a glass replacement company. Bully, a Chihuahua, is his dog.

Woofman, Mary Ann: Woof's grandmother.

Wynne, Sandy: Cat's assistant and computer whiz. Jack, a Jack Russell Terrier, is her dog.

CHARACTERS, CANINE

- Blur: Mel's black Labrador Retriever.
- Brisbane: Nell's red Australian Shepherd.
- Bully: Woof's fawn Chihuahua.
- Cinnamon & Nutmeg: Jennifer's Cavalier King Charles.
- Jack: Sandy's Jack Russell Terrier.
- Max & Maxine: Uncle G's Deputy German Shepherds.
- Renny: Aunt Char's champion Cavalier King Charles Spaniel.
- Champ: Star Bat Dog. A black Labrador Retriever. Owned and trained by Michael O'Donnell.
- Sal: Gabby's Saluki.
- Stallone: Amanda's Bassett Hound.

CHAPTER I

Multimillion-Dollar Baseball Card Stolen!

Headlines like that sold newspapers—lots of newspapers. As the editor-in-chief and executive producer of KDOG, Barkview's premier newspaper, digital TV, and cable network, I should be celebrating. If only I hadn't been sworn to secrecy.

My name is Cat Hawl, and I have a thing about secrets—uncovering them, that is. Keeping them challenges my core reporter's values. That front-page controversy surrounded the Candy Catcher baseball card made it even worse. What really happened that fateful June 1952 night when fire destroyed all but one of the Fab Five's baseball cards?

You bet I wanted to know. So, when Amanda Manley, the executive director of Barkview's baseball card museum, called me three days before the baseball game celebrating Barkview's centennial, I figured she had something important to share. "What do you have?" Forget niceties. Amanda's type-A personality preferred getting right to the point.

"Y-you've got to help me." Panic, pure and simple, came right through the phone.

I straightened from comfy slouch to perfect posture in my executive chair. "Are you all right?"

"Yes. I mean no. The card's been s-stolen." Amanda's voice cracked.

I sucked in my breath. No need to ask which card. Barkview's centennial celebration revolved around the unveiling of one card. So did the National Baseball Card Collectors gala. Even Champ, the bat dog, a nationally-recognized black Labrador Retriever who fetched hitters' baseball bats, already appeared at events to build the hype. Did I mention that Barkview is the dog-friendliest city in America? In this town, designated leash lanes lead to hound playgrounds, and everyone has a BFF (best furry friend) except me. I don't hate dogs. In fact, over the years, I've developed a true appreciation for that special human-canine bond. Is there a right one for me? Perhaps. Let's just say, I'm a work in progress.

"The display case has been smashed. There's a Louisville Slugger and that bat dog's necklace next to it." Amanda's voice trembled. "The c-card is gone."

"The card?" My mind wasn't wrapping around this yet.

My shriek brought Sandy Wynne, my millennial production assistant, running into my office. Jack, her Jack Russell Terrier, jumped like a spring-loaded bobblehead at her feet.

"Are you okay?" Sandy held her tablet like a weapon she would use to defend herself.

I changed my phone to speaker. No sense hiding information from my own personal Watson.

"I don't know how it happened. The alarm was disabled." I pictured Amanda's manicured, blood-red nails yanking through her pixie-cut hair.

"What's Uncle G's opinion?" He'd have one. He always did.

Although he was not technically a blood relative, but rather my Aunt Char's second husband's brother-in-law, I still called the veteran military policeman "Uncle."

"The chief doesn't know. He can't. No one can know. I mean, no one. You need to promise me." Her insistence sounded downright desperate.

"You can't be serious." Gossip moved at the speed of light on the Barkview information superhighway.

"As long as the baseball card is back before its official unveiling on Saturday after the opening-day game…"

My intuition reacted to the catch in her voice. "That's seventy-two hours from now." Unless the game went into extra innings. "Disappointed collectors can be handled."

"Not Clark. He's circling like a vulture, waiting for the opportunity to shut down the museum and repossess all of his family's baseball memorabilia." Amanda's voice shook.

The vision of Clark Sugarland, the current President of Canine Caramel and director of the baseball museum, with his long neck and beaklike nose ready to swoop, stuck in my head. "What? Why?" Since its inception in 1925, Canine Caramel had issued short-run baseball cards that had been sold like the more common bubblegum-accompanied cards, only with their famous caramels. The collection was a true piece of Barkview's storied past and drew year-round visitors to town.

"I don't know. He made a stink about the security. Here in Barkview? It's, like, the safest place in the world."

Apparently, not today. Sandy handed me her tablet. The Candy Catcher baseball card's value flashed at me. I gasped. I couldn't help myself. "That baseball card is worth millions?" An old baseball card of a catcher who'd only played three seasons in the majors? How was that even possible?

"Yeah, I know. The Fabulous Five were the only college team with a season batting average over .500 ever." She let

3

that sink in before adding, "The museum is on the stadium's security system. It's top of the line."

For protecting baseball bats and trophies maybe, but a pocket-sized, million-dollar baseball card? My husband, the security expert, would have an opinion on this for sure. "What kind of alarm did Clark want?"

"A display case with motion and infrared sensors."

Like the one we'd used when the Shepard Diamond had been loaned from the Smithsonian to Barkview as part of our Founder's Day celebration two years ago. Not that it had helped then.

Amanda's regret came out in a ragged breath. "I honestly thought his demand was just another delay tactic. We'd been promised that baseball card for months. Now, I wonder if he knew something."

"Like what?" What wasn't she telling me?

"I don't know. Baseball card collectors can be a nefarious lot."

"Dangerous baseball card collectors?" Was that really a thing? I remembered my father's pride when he'd shown me his boyhood collection stuffed in a dilapidated shoebox in the hall closet.

"Absolutely. You'd be surprised at the offers I get for the cards in our collection."

Not all of them legal, I assumed. A question to ask Clark, subtly. "What exactly do you want me to do? Prove that the dog did it?"

"Yes. I mean, no. I don't care who did it. Just get the card back before Clark finds out. I need to clean up. The museum opens in an hour."

"Wait! No! I need to see the crime scene." Find a missing card with no evidence? "I'm on my way. Don't touch anything..."

That stretch of silence before her agreement concerned me. I needed to hurry. I pushed back my office chair and skirted my monstrosity of a desk. An actual shrine to a nineteenth-century English library, my office hadn't measurably changed since the first Barklay editor-in-chief had proofed copy at this very desk. Although each subsequent occupant had left their mark, like the crystal vase filled with fresh sunflowers left by Aunt Char, I planned to do a much-needed modernization. Neutral paint and, dare I admit it, a TV would help. We needed to enter the twenty-first century already.

Tell that to the long list of remodelers unwilling to touch a splinter in these hallowed halls. Why couldn't they understand that five Pulitzers meant we needed to adapt to continue the tradition? Listen to me, the last living techno dinosaur, advocating for progress.

Seventy-two hours to secretly find a multimillion-dollar baseball card in a town packed with cutthroat collectors. Talk about challenging.

"Champ's owner didn't do this." Sandy's emphatic defense, followed by Jack's bark, refocused me.

"Probably not, but someone wants us to believe he was involved." One look at my dry-clean-only slacks and I wished I'd dressed in comfy jeans and a blue-and-white-striped Barkview Barkers baseball jersey like Sandy. Her attire not only advertised her community support but also made practical sense.

"Why?" Sandy asked.

I shrugged. She knew everything I knew now.

"Do you really think Clark would...?" Sandy asked.

The fourth-generation candymaker could use more sweetener in the get-along-with-others category, but steal his father's baseball card? I flashed her Aunt Char's you-can't-be-serious look. It worked. Sandy shuffled her feet.

"Technically, Ella owns the baseball card. Her grandma willed it to her," Sandy reminded me.

Fifteen-year-old Carmella, or Ella, as she preferred to be called, had a lot of her what's-right-is-right grandma in her. She'd need that resilience to take her place in the family's caramel business. Since Aunt Char had been named the executor of Kandy Sugarland's, Grandma K to most folks around Barkview, will until Ella's twenty-fifth birthday, I knew far more about the family's private affairs than most.

"How did the Candy Catcher's sister end up with the baseball card?" Sandy asked.

I shrugged. "She was the executor of her brother's will."

"Which is odd, too." Sandy hated it when things didn't add up—not that I blamed her in this case. Why had Karl Sugarland, the Fab Five's famous Candy Catcher, appointed his twin sister his executor instead of his son and heir? There had to be some secret there.

"Grandma K passed months ago. Why did Clark insist the card be released now?"

That I understood. "Unveiling the 1952 rookie card at the team's hundred-year baseball celebration is good PR for Canine Caramel."

Sandy huffed, unimpressed. The VIP baseball card collectors, who were already filling the Old Barkview Inn in preparation to view the uncirculated baseball card, disagreed.

"Fans love Champ. Just look at these pictures." Sandy glanced toward the there-ought-to-be-a-TV-there wall before handing me her tablet.

The black Lab, dressed in a blue shirt with a bling-worthy "C" pendant swinging on a chain around his neck and a Louisville Slugger proudly balanced in his mouth, filled the screen. Even more of a fan favorite than anticipated, I realized as I scrolled through the photos. The dog really did make the perfect master of ceremonies. His saintly patience impressed me. Kids yanking on his ears and riding him like a pony only widened his doggy grin. "Michael O'Donnell did a great job training Champ."

"He started throwing mini-bats when the puppy was eight weeks old," Sandy explained.

Even I knew Labs were genetic retrievers. "Is it any wonder his dog-training company is doing well?" Michael's talents would be in high demand in a town like Barkview, where dogs outnumbered people by forty percent.

"I don't think you'll get him to leave North Carolina. You didn't see last night's interview yet, did you?" Sandy asked.

I hated to hurt her feelings. "Not yet. Date night..." I felt my cheeks heat. This newlywed thing messed with my schedule. That's my excuse, and I'm sticking to it.

Sandy's *hmm* communicated understanding and a bit of envy. I don't blame her. Who knew marriage could be so, well, interesting?

"Champ is the most popular star we've had in town in years," Sandy said. "Look at the line for his paw-o-graph."

"His what?" Not another millennial thing? I really couldn't keep up.

There was no missing her eye-roll. "It's a dog's autograph. A paw-o-graph. Get it?"

I got it. Sandy's conclusion appeared right on. The queue circled Barker Field, Barkview's historic baseball field. We'd had celebrity canines before, but never one this popular. I could already see tomorrow's headline: "Champ: Baseball's Newest Bowwow!" Maybe we could keep the missing baseball card a secret.

"Champ wore the 'C' necklace during last night's interview. I'll check with Michael and ask when he noticed it was missing. I'll also start scanning social media for photos to see if

I can pinpoint when he lost it." No further argument. Just action. I liked that about Sandy.

"Limit the timeline as best you can. I'll need the dog's schedule since arrival, too."

Sandy nodded, already tapping on her tablet. "I'll look into Clark, but that answer isn't going to be easy without law enforcement access to personal information."

True. Stealth required subtlety that routine questioning wouldn't allow either. I knew where she was going. My husband wasn't technically a cop, but being a security consultant to both the FBI and local police didn't make him precisely impartial either. His resources might make the ask worth it, though. "I'd better see what's up before I call Russ."

Secrecy amounted to zero if we couldn't find the missing baseball card in time.

CHAPTER 2

Sandy's warning to take pictures of everything stuck with me as I drove east on Oak Street. My amateur shots would be the only crime-scene photos.

Just thinking about Uncle G's zero tolerance for withholding information upset my stomach. The last time I'd tested him, I'd sat desk duty at the station for the holiday weekend. This would be worse, I realized as I turned right on Fifth Street.

Barker Field loomed five blocks ahead of me, cloaked in the coastal fog. The stadium entrance showed off Barkview's Victorian heritage. Constructed from the same sandstone as City Hall, the twin domed towers framing the home-plate grandstands were accented with white gingerbread arches and railings added in the 1920s. The executive-level boxes, added after the Barkers' winning 1963 season, remained leased to their original occupants. Russ had joined that never-moving waitlist a few months ago. Good luck with that. No one gave up baseball seats. Luckily for him, I was willing to share KDOG's.

I skirted the main entrance instead of parking beside Amanda's white Lexus SUV on the south side. The museum occupied all three levels, providing unobstructed views of right field. Except for an occasional foul-ball ricochet requiring glass replacement and cosmetic maintenance, the building hadn't changed in over fifty years.

Amanda stood beside a swaying palm tree near the museum's entrance. One hand on her hip and a paint can in the other, she appeared to be as unmovable as her Basset Hound, Stallone, drooling on her loafers. The woman and her super-sniffing search dog led the county's lost hikers search-and-rescue team. Short and stocky, with a round face framed by her frosted hair, she epitomized my theory that masters choose physically similar canine companions. The brown slacks and white blouse just added to my hypothesis.

"Thank you for coming." Relief softened the lines around Amanda's dark eyes.

As if I'd let her face this alone. We'd been through too much together. "Let's see the crime scene, and I'll help you clean up before the crowds arrive."

"The Candy Catcher card exhibit is closed off until Saturday, but a dozen or so visitors have tried to get a preview. Stallone stopped them. Right, boy?" The dog leaned in for his head scratch.

A Bassett Hound watchdog? Who was I to judge? "I would've guessed more would've tried." The buzz surrounding the one-of-a-kind baseball card had gone national, drawing collectors and enthusiasts from all over.

I caught a whiff of that recognizable fresh paint smell as I followed Amanda through the heavy wood door. Stallone joined us, using the adjacent doggie door, a Barkview staple included in most establishments, including the stadium.

No missing the life-sized bronze of Clark Sugarland's

father, the Candy Catcher, crouched in his catcher's stance. It dominated the marble entry. My knees hurt just looking at it.

A star player at Bark U, Karl had played in the major leagues until his father's sudden death required that he return to Barkview to run the family's candy company. Today his son, Clark, served as the company's CEO and president.

Amanda hip-checked the front door, locked the deadbolt, and headed directly for a velvet rope blocking another door framed in oversized baseball bats. Her key ring clinked as she unlocked it and ordered Stallone to stay. I followed her inside. Glass crunched beneath my feet two steps inside the half-moon-shaped room. That we disturbed evidence bothered me less than the sheer extent of the damage. Morning light streamed through two small half-moon windows, causing the room to glisten. Not in a good way, either. I'd expected the tabletop display to be shattered but not shards of glass to be embedded in the whitewashed wall beside it.

The glass hadn't been hit with precision. Someone had swung for the fences. A shiver traveled the length of my back. This was no random crime of opportunity but a statement.

As I surveyed the crime scene, an eerie sense of familiarity toyed with me. The baseball bat with Champ's flashy "C" beside it had been staged beneath the shattered display case for a reason. Discovering why mattered. I fumbled with my phone and took a picture.

More glass crunched beneath my feet as I circled the room for another photo angle. Something sharp poked my toe. Soft-soled flats weren't exactly the proper footwear for this situation. Amanda offered her shoulder. I held on for balance as I removed a protruding glass sliver.

"We need to sweep up first." Amanda had traded her paint can for a yellow-handled push broom.

"No." The glass patterns needed to be documented and

studied. An experienced investigator would know what to do next. "I'm calling my husband."

"You c-can't," Amanda's voice cracked. "The museum…"

I crushed that objection. "Has bigger issues than a missing baseball card." Amanda's gulp acknowledged it, too. I pressed Russ's speed dial before she convinced me otherwise.

He answered on the second ring. "Good morning, sweetheart." Feeling pooled in my stomach. The husky edge in his voice got me every time.

It felt like forever before I found my words. "We, uh, have a problem."

"What's wrong?" From teasing to focused in a heartbeat. I loved this "we" thing we shared. Being married had serious benefits.

"Meet me at the baseball card museum. I'll explain when you get here. Don't call the chief." I paused on purpose. "Yet." No need to say more. His intuitive mind was already moving chess pieces around on the board. He'd figure it out from my clues. He always did.

His chair scraped across a wood floor. "I'll be there in twenty minutes."

Stress lifted off my shoulders. Another Aunt Char lesson learned: Delegate to those who are more qualified. I felt better already.

Amanda didn't. She gnawed on her lower lip like a dog on a meaty bone. I'd made the right decision—the appropriate decision. Best I refocus us both on the crime scene. "Can you tell me anything about the baseball bat?" The color seemed darker, and the wood grain more pronounced than the bats I'd seen on TV.

"It was made between 1950 and 1961. You can tell because of the inscription." She pointed to the US Patent and Trademark Office information on the base.

"Was it from the museum's 1950s display?" How many 1950s bats were in private collections? I didn't want to know. Yet.

Amanda nodded. "It's the Candy Catcher's bat from the Fabulous Five display. You can tell because the '2' in '125' does not align above the '&' in 'HILLERICH & BRADSBY Co.'"

Amanda knew her baseball bats. No surprise there. That the thief was familiar with the museum's exhibits disturbed me. My intuition cried *Significant!* Coupled with the disabled stadium alarm, this could well be an inside job.

"Why is this card so valuable?" I asked.

"Value is in the eye of the beholder."

"True. But..."

"It's a one-of-a-kind rookie card with a record-setting story," Amanda said. The Fabulous Five Hundred, or Fab Five, were the only college team whose players' collective average exceeded 500. The next best is .396, earned by Delaware State in 1989."

"That's impressive," I said.

"That the Fab Five hit that well or that I knew the answer?" Amanda asked.

"Both. How did this baseball card miraculously survive the caramel factory fire?"

"That's the mystery. Remember, the Fab Five college team was breaking up. The players had all been drafted to different professional teams, so their rookie cards show them in their new respective teams' uniforms. Clark's grandfather intended to release them as an exclusive Barkview homegrown set. He supposedly kept the originals locked in his desk." Amanda took a breath. "That desk was badly burned but restored after the fire. The desk was a replica of the *Resolute* desk in the Oval Office."

"A gift from Queen Victoria to President Hayes." My college

13

history minor finally paid off. And I'd watched the Nicolas Cage movie.

"It's a double-pedestal partners desk he shared with his wife, Dolce."

My chuckle slipped out. "Sweet Sugarland? She must've loved that." And I complained about my name. Maybe being named after an offshore California island wasn't so bad after all.

Amanda's arched brow made me add, "Dolce means sweet in Italian."

"Her family made caramels. The desk is at Barker Field in the general manager's office now. Clark had the desk moved there when his brother took over as the team's general manager."

Nothing nefarious about that. "Getting back to the baseball cards. Were the other cards in the set destroyed in the fire?"

"That was the story, until Grandma K requested that Ella donate the Candy Catcher baseball card to the museum. Over the years, there have been rumors of other cards from the set being bought by anonymous buyers, but no one ever confirmed those stories."

Did the cards exist or not? "Was Nana Dolce actively involved in the candy company?"

"I don't know. Why does it matter?" Amanda asked.

"Did she actually share the desk with her husband, or was it just a courtesy place for her to sit when she visited? Women had different roles back in 1920." A shared desk meant someone else potentially had access to the locked drawers. My pulse thumped. Was it possible the other cards had been spared too? Wouldn't that be a coup? If so, where had they been for the past seventy years? "Where the Candy Catcher baseball card found?"

"Grandma K never said. Ella might know. She has her

grandmother's documents." Then she added, only half under her breath, "Much to Clark's annoyance."

Amanda had worked with Grandma K to establish the museum and had been curator for a decade. That made her an insider.

"Isn't it odd that Grandma K willed the information to her fifteen-year-old granddaughter instead of her nephew who runs the family business?" I asked.

"Clark thinks so. I don't though. Like her mother before her, Grandma K managed Canine Caramel effectively for a long time. Clark is not the leader either his mother or aunt was. Maybe Ella will be someday."

Talk about a loaded response. Defensiveness kicked in. I knew what being compared to an icon felt like. Management styles differed. True, I lacked Aunt Char's calm efficiency, but my seat-of-the-pants style didn't make me a less effective leader.

"Don't take this the wrong way. If Ella's father had survived..." Amanda let my mind fill in the blank.

"He was the Barkview Barkers' GM." The baseball team had consistently won their division under his leadership. "He wasn't involved in the candy company's operation?"

"Not on a daily basis, but Henry served on the board of directors. He wasn't the most diplomatic guy. I don't think he ever candy-coated a thing, but you knew where you stood." Amanda's wistful smile said she'd liked him. Maybe too much. "Probably the only person Clark couldn't push around."

I took my time scribbling a Post-it, my eye on Amanda. Her stiff body language indicated she had more to say. I let the silence stretch between us.

Aunt Char's lessons in patience paid off now. Amanda blurted out, "Clark has threatened to cut our funding."

"Why?" Was there more to Clark's threat to repossess the Sugarland family's baseball memorabilia?

"He said the museum wasn't solvent. We're a 501(c)(3) nonprofit. By definition, we're not allowed to be profitable," Amanda insisted.

Indelicate as it was, I had to ask. "How much money did you lose last year?" Money and motive went together like baseball and hotdogs.

"No more than usual. I think Clark had been counting on getting his hands on Grandma K's money. With your aunt in charge of Ella's share, he can't bully his way out of whatever mess he's in this time."

Now I understood why Grandma K had chosen Aunt Char to be Ella's advocate rather than her trendy, yoga instructor mother. A savvy businesswoman, my aunt would watch over Ella's assets like a mama bear. I needed to protect my aunt from Clark by finding that missing baseball card to ensure her sanity. Time to focus on the evidence. "Was the museum's front door open when you arrived?"

The ends of Amanda's frosted hair swished across her cheeks with her headshake. "No. That's what's so odd. The dead bolt doesn't align right, so you need to push the door just so to close it."

That explained Amanda's earlier hip-check.

"It's on my list to get fixed. Which is beside the point. It was locked when I arrived."

"You're sure?" The bat from the display, Champ's necklace, and the stealth break-in pointed to someone with better than a passing knowledge of the museum.

"Of course, I'm sure. I broke my nail." She poked a ragged cherry-red fingernail toward me. "They didn't use the fire escape door either. I checked."

Although it had been restored, the old building featured

few windows and even fewer doors. More proof of an inside job. "Then how did they get in?"

"I have no idea."

Amanda, stumped? She knew this building better than anyone.

Stallone's loud, baying bark reverberated around us a second before movement in the entry caught my eye. It couldn't be Russ. We'd been locked inside.

Amanda saw it too. Her broom raised like a club, she went to investigate. Impulsively, I grabbed the paint can. A horizontal swing would take anyone out at the hips. In my hurry I collided with Amanda, losing my grip on the handle. Time stopped as the can clanked end over end on the tile and then flipped onto its side, rolling like a gutter ball into the wall. I cringed, waiting for the lid to pop and the paint to splatter everywhere. Thankfully, it didn't. The paint can rolled up against the wall and stopped.

Stallone's deafening bark ended that victory celebration.

"Stallone, down." The Bassett Hound's answering bark drowned out Amanda's screech. He stood up on his hind legs, his front paws on the Catcher's bronze knee, and stretched upward.

Ever seen a Basset Hound climb? My amusement escaped as a snort and kept coming. Until I saw a big, black, Hitchcock-worthy crow perched on the Candy Catcher's left shoulder.

Except for Stallone's ears flapping, pin-dropping silence ensued.

"How did that bird get in here?" I finally asked.

Amanda's ashen complexion indicated something more serious. "It's the bat."

"You have a bat?" I ducked and looked around. I saw only the bird.

"Not a flying bat. It's the Candy Catcher's baseball bat. I

need to get it back in the display." Amanda pivoted, nearly knocking me over in her haste to return to the crime scene.

Not connecting her comments, I blocked her path. "Stop. That bat is evidence. It needs to be properly processed. Checked for fingerprints." Russ would be here soon enough.

Amanda's blink questioned my sanity. "Mine are already all over it. I handle it daily."

"There could be other fingerprints or blood," I said. There was glass everywhere. The perpetrator could've been cut.

"Or not. The crow's a-an omen. The Candy Catcher can't be separated from his bat. He carried it with him to every game day. Even kept it in his office after he retired."

"You can't be serious." Her dead-dog stare said otherwise. I'd heard baseball players and fans tended to be superstitious, but Karl was a statue.

"How else do you explain the crow?" Amanda crossed her arms, adamant.

Granted, a crow generally represented bad luck, but in this case... "The bird could've come in with the perp. Maybe it could show us how they got in."

I waved my arms. The bird's squawk hurt my ears before it took flight, circling the statue and then flying deeper into the museum.

"Follow it!" I shouted.

Stallone waited for Amanda's command and took off after it, lumbering faster than I'd imagined a short-legged dog that size could move. The two trackers had that covered.

My phone rang before I could join them. I knew who it was without looking at the screen. My Aunt Char had a sixth sense when something was up. I swallowed my dread and answered anyway. "Is this a mayoral call or a family call?"

"I need your help at City Hall right away, my dear." No

greeting from the queen of social graces? This couldn't be good.

"What's happened?" I hoped I'd kept any sign of anxiety out of my voice.

"Michael, Champ's handler, is on his way to Barkview Hospital."

"What? Is he okay?" Another crime? Could the day get worse?

"It's nothing life-threatening. I'm guessing it's appendicitis. He'll need immediate surgery."

So much for relief. I felt the leash tugging at me. I knew what that meant.

"I need you to take charge of Champ," Aunt Char announced.

Me, care for a celebrity Labrador Retriever? "You can't be serious. Champ is the most popular star we've had in town in years." The line of people willing to watch the bat dog had to be a mile long, literally.

"Michael insisted. His wife agreed. She wants to be here, but both of her children are ill. They need her more than Michael does. I assured her we would take good care of him. It won't be for long. She'll be here in a few days."

A difficult choice, for sure. "What about Sandy?" She knew everything about that dog.

"Jack's Napoleon complex bears further study." Aunt Char's response proved her diplomatic abilities.

"He barks at everyone," I said.

"He is a Jack Russell. Michael thinks you are the best choice for Champ. The show must go on, you know."

Champ's many upcoming appearances loomed. "Says the man drugged up on pain meds." I checked the time. Good thing I'd already called Russ. He would need to finish processing this crime scene. "I'll be there in fifteen minutes."

"Excellent. I'll hold presenting the Bone to the City to Champ until you arrive."

No pressure there. I ended the call.

"What's happened to Champ?" Amanda had returned from the bird chase and stood beside the bronze statue, stroking Stallone's neck. I hadn't heard her return.

"Champ is fine. His handler is in the hospital. Nothing serious." I changed the subject. "Did you find where the bird came in?"

"Yeah. I need to call Dan Woofman to replace the foul ball window. Someone broke it again." I got her annoyance. "I doubt a person could crawl through that window. It's too high."

Climbing through a window twenty-plus feet above the ground wouldn't be easy, but if the thief was athletic—maybe even a gymnast—it was possible. I'd seen what they could do when the Shepard Diamond had been stolen out of the Old Barkview Inn's Crown Room.

"This hundred-year baseball celebration is jinxed," Amanda announced. "The crow proves it."

Much as I wanted to argue, her prophetic words resonated. The centerpiece for the celebration had been stolen and the master of ceremonies' handler hospitalized. "It's nothing we can't handle." I meant it too. Barkview had come through worse.

"I am dead-dog serious. After the fire, Karl promised not to release a 1952 card set."

I felt a strange foreboding. "We're not releasing a set. No one can. The other four cards were destroyed."

Amanda's eyes shone like high-quality tiger's eyes. "What if those cards weren't lost in the fire? Don't you see? Displaying the Candy Catcher card breaks his word."

In a roundabout sort of way, maybe. I'd not take odds on that ruling. "That's a whole lot of supposition."

"No secret is safe from fate."

How well I knew the fickle nature of secrets. They did ultimately reveal themselves, but they did it on their own timeline. The likelihood of finding four cards believed destroyed after seventy years seemed hardly discussion-worthy. If Amanda was right though, we had a multimillion-dollar motive.

CHAPTER 3

I waited for Russ in the parking lot prepared to brief him. He waited for my complete explanation before he gathered me in a warm embrace and whispered, "I got this."

Of course he did. Relief rolled off my shoulders. It bothered me only slightly that he'd do a far better job sorting evidence and charming information out of Amanda anyway.

"It means we'll have a hairy, shedding Labrador Retriever in the house." I cringed just thinking about his watery red eyes and sneezing fits. "You can say no."

He laughed off my warning. "Relax. I'll be fine. I'm surrounded by dogs every day. I'm getting used to it."

Or not. My biggest fear had to be him rolling over one morning and deciding I wasn't worth it. I yoga-breathed. We were married. He was legally required to be there.

Refusing to give Amanda an out, I escorted him inside the museum before climbing into my car and driving the five long blocks to City Hall.

Constructed from local sandstone brick with a pitched roof and elegant redwood accents, City Hall epitomized the unique elegance that was Barkview. Although it was never easy to park downtown, a single trip around the block usually netted a recently vacated spot. Not today, which said a lot about the crowd gathered for the Bone to the City presentation. I glanced at the time. Already late. Forget parking karma, I'd have to create my own.

Executive decision made, I parked behind Aunt Char's Mercedes, blocking her and her assistant's exit. Urgent city business called. Not that the police chief would buy that excuse. He'd ticketed me for failure to yield to an oncoming Pekingese last year. Yes, a lick-it ticket.

This time the fine would be warranted, I decided as I trotted up the sandstone steps. One look at the restless crowd and their equally impatient canines confirmed that the number of occupants in the grand foyer tested the fire department's capacity rules.

Sandy met me at the door. Using her tablet as a barrier, she miraculously cleared a path across the parquet floor to the podium set up between the elegant oak double staircases. Aunt Char's smile thanked me as she stepped up to the microphone. Dressed in a classic Dior suit, her blonde hair swept back, she looked more like a reigning Nordic monarch than a beach city mayor. Renny, her champion Cavalier King Charles Spaniel, sat at her regal best beside the podium.

My aunt's nod directed me to the left where a midnight-black Labrador Retriever dressed in a royal-blue baseball jersey sat sphinx-style with his paws stretched out in front of him. Without a bat in his mouth or the "C" necklace around his neck, Champ looked like any other mellow black Lab I'd ever met. But then his intense black gaze met mine. I suddenly understood exactly why he was a star. It wasn't the dog's well-defined facial structure or shiny, midnight coat. It was his remarkable focus. While the antsy crowd noise, the playful barking and shuffling distracted me, tail straight and ears alert, Champ saw nothing but me. Me!

I gulped. Irrational intimidation froze me solid. Control this dog? He'd have me wrapped around his paw in no time. I swear every doubting eye, human and canine, locked on me.

Renny's single bark ended my meltdown. I'd been in way scarier situations before.

Taking charge isn't about conquering my fear of failure.
It's knowing that failure isn't an option.

The reminder kicked my practical mind into action. Labrador Retrievers were working dogs who thrived on doing their job. Champ knew what to do, and so did I. I met the Lab's gaze straight on and pointed to the podium. "Champ, come."

Tail wagging, the dog obeyed.

Test passed. I smiled. The Cavalier King Charles's haughty I-told-you-so head toss barely registered. Sometimes it took a reminder.

"I'll set up the ink pad beside the baseball cards and the caramels next to the podium. Give each person a caramel with their signed card." Sandy displayed a one-inch beige caramel wrapped in end-twisted Canine Caramel–printed cellophane.

"Are these the same caramels the original Fab Five baseball cards would've been sold with?" I asked.

"Yup. It's the hundred-year-old recipe." Sandy handed me a blue backpack and a Champ-size baseball cap. "If you could get him to wear this, it'll look good for the photo op afterward."

I snapped the black elastic strap. So, that's how the super-cute cap stayed on the dog's head. Not exactly cushy-comfortable. Good luck getting *any* dog to stand still for this, never mind a particular star.

"I'll try. No promises." I should've asked what to do with the ink pad, but Aunt Char started the presentation. "Good afternoon and welcome. We are here today to welcome Champ…"

Applause erupted, echoing in the rotunda and drowning out my aunt's words. Sandy had been right on about the black Lab's popularity. Barkview had a new fan favorite.

Champ sat at attention for the entire ten-minute ceremony. When Aunt Char offered him the twelve-inch-long silver bone, the bat dog accepted it and posed like a statuesque long-horned sheep atop the mountain. He barely blinked despite what felt like a hundred I-see-stars flashes.

Champ waited for my signal before returning to my side. He dropped the bone at my feet and nudged the baseball cap in my hand. And I'd thought inducing him to wear the hat would be an issue. A dog that just stands there asking to be tortured? Except for my husband sneezing his head off from allergy-inducing Labrador dander, this dog-sitting gig looked like it would be a dink over the center field fence.

The black elastic blended into the dog's fur after I slipped it under his chin. Champ scanned the room and then looked at me, seeming to say, "Get ready." For what? A couple of pictures and…

The floodgates might as well have opened the way the crowd swelled toward us, demanding to pet and to pose for a picture with Champ. Not one or two people, but the whole audience waved baseball cards, Champ-printed T-shirts, and baseball caps to be autographed. A designer BOGO free-for-all couldn't be more chaotic. When a fan bumped me aside, I jerked back, suddenly attacked by in-your-face heebie-jeebies.

Champ sat at attention, his tail sticking straight out behind him while he flashed his doggy grin. He nosed my hand until I dropped the ink pad. He stepped on the silver case and looked at me with his big black eyes.

I got it. We both had a job to do. If he could persevere with hundreds of people hanging all over him... I scooped up the inkpad, opened it, and set it on the ground beside the dog's front paw. Champ stepped on the pad and the first baseball card. His pawprint filled the back side of the card, obscuring parts of his dog story. Not a big issue. Everyone pretty much knew it anyway. Like an old-time postal employee canceling mail, Champ signed his paw-o-graphs again and again.

Watching a pro in action, I marveled at the dog's poise and patience. I think Champ even had a sixth sense to protect his tail. Twice I saw him move a split second before someone would've stepped on it.

I don't know how long we remained in that exact spot, interacting with fans until Aunt Char announced Champ's next appearance at the pregame Beach Bash opening tonight. I groaned, just thinking about another dog and pony show.

The bat dog pressed up against my thigh. Was he trying to comfort me? I couldn't help but stroke and praise him. What an amazing dog. I hunted for treats in his logoed black back-pack. Nothing. I went in for a deeper dive. There had to be a snack in here somewhere. Renny would've gone on strike thirty minutes ago without proper chicken treat motivation.

Still no treats. How was that possible? Unless Champ only expected praise for his efforts. It seemed unfair.

"Well done. Both of you." Aunt Char also stroked Champ from head to tail. The dog shimmied in pleasure.

"Champ's incredible!" Every word came from my heart.

Aunt Char smiled. "That he is. Don't forget, my dear, that Champ is still a dog."

"Not like any dog I've ever dog-sat for." Gem, Ariana's German Shepherd, who'd helped me find the Shepard

26

Diamond, had also been well-trained. That dog had spent our time together herding me into safe corners. Champ didn't push me around at all. I liked that a lot.

"He's exactly like every dog you've sat for." I heard Aunt Char's warning. I really did. I just didn't believe it. I'd just spent over an hour with the best dog ever.

Sandy came up behind me. "Great job." She rubbed Champ's back. He rolled over for her. Feet in the air, the Lab did look more doggish.

"I'm sure Champ could use a rest before tonight's event," Aunt Char said.

I nodded. I could use one too. I didn't want to worry her about the missing baseball card but still needed to ask. "Did Clark or Ella finally give the Candy Catcher card to the museum?"

I tried to ignore Aunt Char's raised brow. "Ella did. Grandma K left the card to her."

I hated to put Aunt Char, the executor of Grandma K's will, in a compromising situation. Still, I needed to know. "Why did it take so long for Ella to donate it?"

"You will need to ask Ella," Aunt Char replied. "Why do you ask?"

I glanced around the foyer. Although it had mostly emptied, people still passed through the space to transact normal city business. I shook my head. No one could overhear this conversation.

Aunt Char nodded her understanding. "Ella's classes will let out at 2:30. I will tell her that you and Champ will be picking her up and taking her to the stadium today. She will be thrilled. Her chocolate Labrador passed a month after her father."

That sounded traumatic. The black Lab leaned against me. He acknowledged his name with a head bob. "The stadium?" I asked.

"Yes. She's quite the baseball fan." The twinkle in Aunt Char's eye promised a revelation she did not intend to share. A secret I needed to draw out of a fifteen-year-old. Great.

Sandy followed me outside, carrying another nylon duffle bag bulging, no doubt, with Champ's toys and food. Her "how to care for Champ" lecture did not disappoint.

"Labs in general are pretty chill, provided you throw something for them to fetch. Make sure you play with him before you bring him to the Beach Bash. Just because he's so well behaved doesn't mean that he's not a dog."

I glanced at the Lab watching me with his dark eyes and heeling perfectly at my side. Seriously? "Are you trying to tell me that he's going to transform into a barking runaway or something?"

Sandy's chuckle relaxed me. "No. But he's entitled to dog time too." She reached down Champ's back, pulled the baseball jersey over his head, and stuffed it in his goodie bag.

The Lab puppy-shook, the quiver traveling the length of his body like a mini-tremor.

"The jersey is his cue that it's time to work. Make sure you put it on him before you get to his appearances," Sandy said. "I loaded all the events on your calendar with thirty-minute reminders on your phone. I also put a list of Champ's commands in the duffle. A few are unique. Learn them. You wouldn't want to confuse our star."

What about me? I thought dog commands were universal. Ugh! I scratched Champ's head. He licked my hand. "No problem. We'll be fine. He's the most well-behaved dog I've ever met."

"Go with that, then," Sandy replied.

Yet another warning? What did Sandy know that I didn't? "You should send Jack to Michael's dog-training school. If you could stop his barking..." Sandy's clenched jaw stopped my commentary. What was I thinking, passing judgment on her baby? "I'm sorry. I didn't mean... It's none of my business."

"Yes, you did, and you're right. Jack's overprotective."

But she liked that about the dog. How many times did I need to remind myself that Jack wasn't my choice? He was Sandy's match.

"Michael did tell me that he noticed Champ's necklace was missing when he got back to his hotel room at the Old Barkview Inn last night after nine," Sandy added. "I'm not sure he was thinking clearly when I asked, though."

I pictured her leaning over the gurney as the paramedics rushed him to the ambulance. "Don't tell me..."

"You'd have done the same."

I had to admire her righteous pride. I'd trained her well. "That's a little over an hour window. Who did Champ interact with between the studio and his hotel room?" Arriving after nine meant that Will Oldeman, my eyes and ears at the Old Barkview Inn, had already gone off duty before Champ had returned.

"Michael said no one stopped him on the walk from the studio to the hotel, but he was mobbed in the lobby. He mentioned a guy with a black cowboy hat. I'll ask around. How many black cowboy hats can there be at the Old Barkview Inn during a baseball card convention?"

Good point. During the Rodeo, I'd take the odds.

"Do you need me to pick up Ella or go see Amanda?" Sandy asked.

"Russ is with Amanda right now," I replied.

"I knew you'd call him," Sandy said.

Was I getting that predictable? "It was the right thing to do." No need for me to defend myself. "We'll meet later to

29

compare notes, at my house after tonight's show. See what you can find about the other Fab Five baseball cards in the set."

"Find out what? Do you think there's a chance those cards weren't destroyed in the fire?" I recognized that treasure-hunter gleam in Sandy's sapphire-blue eyes. "They'd be worth a fortune."

"No kidding. I wish I knew if they were still intact. It seems odd that only one card survived." My intuition told me nothing.

"I agree. I'll look deeper into the fire," Sandy promised.

Her lotto-fever enthusiasm was contagious. "Since Ella has Grandma K's papers, I'm hoping she can tell me more."

I checked the time. Not enough to visit Canine Caramel's downtown factory, but... "I have an hour before Ella's classes let out. I think I'll walk to the Daily Wag for a sandwich." At gossip central's unofficial headquarters, the coffeeshop owner, Gabby Turner, molded public opinion one espresso at a time.

"You might want to move your car first," Sandy suggested. "Officer Richards arrived five minutes ago with his ticket book out."

My double-parked car! I took off at a run. Champ's gear bag bounced off my hip as the Lab and I matched strides down the steps and around the sandstone building. No sign of our All-American police officer had to be good news. Maybe I'd gotten lucky. I kept up the pace until I saw the telltale rectangular paper beneath my windshield wiper, flapping in the afternoon breeze. Talk about deflating.

I slowed to a walk, sucking in big gulps of air. Playing pickleball three times a week made running short spurts easy. Longer distances, not so much. Champ simply adjusted to my pace without judgment. Walking this medium-sized dog had to be less stressful than running after my aunt's fifteen-pound, mush-dog Cavalier. Loading him into my car... I opened the passenger door and pointed to the seat. "In."

Champ glanced at the seat and back at me, his slow black-eyed blink making me feel like I'd spoken Greek.

Maybe I had. I reached into Champ's bag for the command list Sandy had prepared for me. Who knew I'd need it this soon? I scanned the sheet. "Load up."

The black Lab leaped inside. Note to self: *memorize the command list*. No need for a Post-it, either, I realized, as I walked toward the driver's side.

"You missed him by two minutes." Danny Woofman, "Woof" to us all, and his beach-blond surfer's do popped up from the side of Aunt Char's sedan. Dressed in a not-quite-white lab coat and faded blue jeans, he looked more like a laid-back college professor than a precision glass replacer. Beside him, his pint-sized fawn-colored Chihuahua, Bully, guarded the bumper like a Doberman.

I jumped at least a foot. "Geez, Woof."

"Sorry. Didn't mean to scare you. Your aunt wanted the rock nick in her windshield repaired." He pointed to a small crack in the glass. "I figured it was a good excuse to meet Champ."

"You were inside?" I didn't recall seeing him. In all fairness, the crowd had been overwhelming.

"Yeah. In the back. Too many people to get a Champ base-ball card."

"No problem." I removed a signed card from my pouch. When Bully's big-dog growl showed a full set of needle-sharp teeth, I pulled back the Champ card. The contrast between muscle-bound, gentle giant Woof and this mighty mouse, Bully, contradicted my theory that dogs and their humans matched in looks and behavior. In my defense, Woof had inherited Bully from his mother, who now resided in a memory-care facility. Woof had risen to the occasion. Bully reminded me of a dashboard bobblehead, the way the Chihuahua's narrow head, longish nose, and large black eyes bobbed as they stared at me.

"Be nice." Woof set the dog onto his shoulder, out of reach. I still eyed the mini dog as I handed him the baseball card.

"Thank you," said Woof.

"Are you a collector?" Maybe finding a baseball card collector wasn't going to be too difficult.

"Not really. I'm on the committee to hire the Barkers' bat dog. The dog-friendliest city in America should have a bat dog."

I'd wondered about that. "I agree. Come see me next week. We'll do a few news spots on it."

Woof smiled. "Thank you. Champ just being here will help."

I had to agree with that. "Did Amanda call you?"

"Yeah. She says the foul-ball window needs replacement. Second repair already this season."

"The season hasn't started yet," I said.

"Practice started a few weeks ago. It'll take real talent to beat my dad's window breaking record."

The pride in his voice surprised me. Who wanted to be remembered as the hitter who broke the most foul-ball windows? "Forty-something, right?"

"Forty-eight during the 1984 season." Woof's smile had to be an inside joke. "Inspired Dad to start the glass business when he retired his bat. I pitched the stadium grounds group about changing the window to plexiglass. No interest."

"Why not?" Replacing windows wasn't cheap.

"Tradition, I suppose. My dad called it a pincher's bucket." He must've seen my confusion. "The batter who breaks the window buys the team a round. My dad about went broke."

32

I smiled. This would make a good story for the *Bark View*. "You played ball too, right?"

"Division I, 2005 to 2009. Never made it to the big leagues."

His wistfulness surprised me. "You coach Little League. You carry on your family's tradition every season."

Woof wiped his hands with a white cloth. "Thank you for saying so. I told Officer Richards you had Champ duty today."

"Thank you." Not that it had helped. I lifted the ticket. Bold letters caught my eye, spelling out "Champ's Parking Pass." A freebie for me? This dog really was a celebrity.

CHAPTER 4

I could have left my car where it was, but in the end, I drove across the street and parked in the Daily Wag's lot. No sense pressing my luck.

The corner Victorian, built in 1907 in the classic, white-washed gingerbread style, celebrated our baseball centennial with historic pennants draped from the lattice and colorful tulips in bat-shaped vases centered on the wrought iron tables.

The warm afternoon sun brought the crowd outside, or maybe it was Champ. The spindle railed porch had been vacant when I arrived, but now people spilled out on both sides of the door. The path leading to the counter might as well have been a red carpet the way twenty people crowded the edge, requesting selfies. Champ stoically posed as requested until a growling Miniature Pinscher made his ear twitch.

Dogfight avoidance my top priority, I ended the publicity session and hip-bumped my way past a Standard Poodle. I stepped over two Dachshunds and brushed a Golden Retriever's butt enroute to the antique cash register.

"Good afternoon, Cat. Champ." Gabby's warm brown eyes

and I'm-your-best-friend smile encouraged confidences. Dressed in a blue Barkview Barkers striped jersey, with her dark hair hidden beneath the team's baseball cap, she looked so much like her Saluki, Sal, that I blinked. True owner-dog look-alikes, the pair's lanky, angular features brought a strung-out caffeine junkie to mind.

Gabby handed me a tall paper cup dusted with dark chocolate. The aroma of steaming caramel cappuccino teased me as I took a long, satisfying swallow.

Gabby's smile widened. "I swear you purr when you drink that."

"Don't tell anyone." The wrong thing to say to the director of gossip central.

Today she only shrugged and leaned over the marble countertop. She offered Champ a pup's cup, the Daily Wag's whipped cream treat. The Lab caught the black-and-white paw-printed paper cup with his tongue. In one lick he cleaned the cup and flipped it back onto the counter, right side up, a smear of white cream on his snout the only evidence of his treat. Then he took a bow.

If I hadn't seen it, I'd never have believed it. Gabby didn't either. Speechlessness had to be unfamiliar territory for her. Tonight's headline eluded even me.

A chant of "Champ" erupted all around us.

Gabby recovered first. "Well, that was something."

"Sure was," I admitted. I scratched Champ's head as I looked up at the menu. "Let me have a turkey club and a..." The sweet potato fries called me, but... "A side salad." Champ nudged my thigh. He didn't like that choice either.

Gabby smothered a smile. She'd seen it all. Great.

I tapped my credit card on the pay terminal. "Something I should know about?"

Gabby could always be counted on for outrageous fodder.

The telltale twinkle in her dark-roast-brown eyes promised a zinger. "W-e-l-l." She motioned me toward a quiet corner. "I'll bring your sandwich over in a minute."

Like any part of this coffee shop offered privacy. I'd come in for information. No reason to stop now. Coffee in hand, Champ and I settled at the indicated table. The Lab waited for me to sit before stretching across my feet and closing his eyes. After the morning I'd had, I thought maybe I'd join him...until I smelled bacon.

My mouth watered as Gabby crossed the shop with my sandwich. Of course, my phone rang as she placed the plate on the table. "It's Russ. I need to take this."

Gabby pointed at my lipstick-stained coffee. "Refill?"

I nodded. Not wanting the entire coffee shop to hear my conversation with my husband, I slipped my foot from beneath the snoring Lab, walked a few steps to the side door, and slipped outside onto the porch. "Everything okay?"

"Yes. I've convinced Amanda that we need the chief's resources. Meet us at police headquarters—"

"I'm picking up Ella at 2:30."

"Make it 5 p.m. We can compare notes then. Love you."

He hung up before I could respond. I crushed my annoyance that he'd positively done a better job with Amanda than me. This wasn't a competition between us. We worked better together.

The entire call had lasted two minutes. I'd even beaten Gabby to the table with my coffee refill. Champ hadn't moved either by the time I slipped back into my chair and reached for my sandwich. I bit into the crusty sourdough bread and tasted crunchy lettuce, ripe tomato, and avocado. No bacon, no turkey, no cheese. What? I lifted the bread. Sure enough, only garden vegetables.

Gabby handed me another coffee as she slid into the chair. "How's the club?"

"You forgot the meat." I didn't mean to growl.

"What? I put the bacon on myself. I smelled it walking over here."

So had I. I showed her the bare sandwich. We glanced at the snoring Lab beneath the table at the same time. "No way. The bread wasn't even disturbed," I said.

Gabby leaned down. "Aha! A bacon bit." She dropped a minuscule piece of bacon on the plate. "We've found our thief."

Champ opened his eyes and blinked in pure innocence.

"Don't fall for those puppy-dog eyes." Gabby's remark made Champ sit up. "Star or not, you've been caught with your paws in the treat jar."

Champ hung his head. His pout touched my heart. I had to defend him. "It's my fault. I shouldn't have left him alone with food within his reach."

Gabby wasn't ready to let it go. I probably shouldn't either, but he was a celebrity dog. "I'll just go vegan today. Lesson learned. I'll protect my meal better next time." I'd been warned that he was a dog—a dog with a sneaky meat habit.

Champ settled at my feet again, but not until he snagged that last bit of bacon.

Gabby shook her head. "You're too soft-hearted."

Me? I took another bite of my sandwich. Really, it wasn't too bad, just not what I'd expected. "Tell me what you know."

Refocused, Gabby's smile promised a lot. "Well. Rumor has it, Clark's holding invoices."

"You mean not paying his vendors on time?" A common strategy for someone short of cash.

"Yup. The pumpkin caramels didn't do so well last year."

"Really? Pumpkin everything is the thing, isn't it?" Or so I'd been told. Not my choice.

"I know. I sold more pumpkin lattes than I ever had. Clark fudged the quality. I sold the four-pack pumpkin and spice caramels at the counter. The cheap imported packaging didn't fit the high-end candies. I told Clark it fell apart before I bagged it. He blamed me for spilling coffee on it. My sales were one and done. I had to discount the last packages to get rid of them."

An influencer before they were a thing, Gabby bad-mouthing a product tanked sales. "I'm not a pumpkin fan. I didn't try it," I admitted.

"I wasn't the only one. Ask anyone else who sold it," Gabby said.

An underperforming holiday candy launch would hurt the company financially, but was that enough to cause Clark to close the baseball museum? "I'll talk to him." How did you ask someone if they were in financial trouble?

"I doubt it's anything too serious. I mean, Canine Caramel's been around for a hundred years. They do need an update at the factory. Their equipment could be on the Antiques Roadshow," Gabby said.

I chuckled. "That old?"

"Yeah. It dates back to the 1950s and 1960s. I took their historic plant tour last year."

"Clark isn't a big fan of change," I said.

"His son is. Jordan's all about technology," Gabby replied.

Had to be a generational thing. Time to change the topic. "Do you know any baseball card collectors?"

"Sure. Why?"

So much for subtlety. Gabby suspected something. Her mind racing with possibilities scared me. Even Gabby's dog watched me squirm.

"I don't understand why the Candy Catcher's card is so valuable," I said quickly. Which was true. "After leaving

Barkview, Candy Catcher only played in the majors for three years. He didn't win any grand titles there. It makes no sense."

Gabby relaxed. "It's not about the card. It's the story and the exclusivity."

I'd heard that before. "I still don't understand."

Gabby in lecture mode meant information overload. "The Fab Five won the NCAA title. They were All-Americans, and every one of them was drafted into the majors. That's never happened before or since. The baseball cards represented a once-in-a-lifetime phenomenon."

"But one guy never played in the majors." I couldn't remember all the details. They hadn't seemed important at the time.

"That's why it was so crazy. It was like the cards were jinxed."

"Jinxed?" Gabby had my attention now, and clearly everyone else's, since pin-dropping silence ensued as every ear in the room tuned in. So much for a private table. "Why?"

She planted her elbows on the table and leaned in whisper-close. "The baseball cards were created from hand-painted color reproductions of the original black-and-white photos." She paused for effect.

It worked. I waited.

"Nana Dolce's mother painted them."

"So?" She wasn't Rembrandt.

"In 1952. Come on, Cat. The woman was born in the 1800s. Her skill was amazing considering what she had to work with. It was too bad the printing plates were destroyed after the production run."

"Karl got what he wanted. The baseball cards turned out to be a very limited edition," I agreed.

"And Nana Dolce's mother was too old to repaint them.

She passed in 1953. My granny attended to her. You remember she was a doctor?"

How could I forget my harrowing experience in the tunnel we'd found at Gabby's grandmother's old medical office?

"Nana Dolce's mama was a talented artist who never got a chance because of time and place. The baseball cards were her legacy to her grandson."

A good story. "So, why are the cards jinxed?" I asked.

"I'm getting to that. The fire occurred the day after the production runs arrived at the factory. The cards were scheduled to be released the following week. The night of the fire, Owen Daniels, the star first baseman, was in a car accident. He shattered his ankle. He walked with a limp for the rest of his life. My granny treated his burns at Barkview Hospital."

My intuition twinged. "I've never heard that. How do you know he was burned?"

"The hospital reports don't say anything about burns, but my granny's treatment notes do," Gabby insisted.

"What happened to the car?"

"Not a scratch on it according to Granny."

This was sounding more and more like a cover up. "Were any of the other players injured?"

"Not that Granny recorded, but the Candy Catcher supposedly caught influenza and Bertie Wallace, the third baseman, contracted acute bronchitis the day after the fire."

"Respiratory issues..." I paused. Gabby's thought process had merit. Maybe too much. "Perhaps related to smoke inhalation?"

"Don't know for sure. Neither went to Granny for care. The part Granny talked about was that the Fab Five went their separate ways after the fire. Some say Owen held the team together. Granny thought there was more to it. Owen started drinking after the accident, and his girlfriend took off."

"The man's life changed that day. A little depression seems normal," I said.

"A little, yeah. Granny said it went on for years."

"Guilt-driven?" Had the caramel factory fire been the result of a college prank gone wrong?

"What did your granny think happened to the other original baseball cards?" I asked, but I knew.

"After the catcher's card was discovered, she wondered if the rest had really been destroyed."

I joined in the collective gasp. Like information on the internet, if Gabby said it, it had to be true.

Could it be that four priceless baseball cards were waiting to be found? The big question was, who else knew it, and how far would they go to find them?

CHAPTER 5

I arrived at Barkview High to pick up Ella a few minutes before the end-of-the-day bell and waited in the mile-long line of SUVs in front of the two-story sandstone building. Originally built in 1903 to house the university's veterinary school, it had been converted into a high school in the 1950s and remodeled so many times since then that only the outer walls remained original. Inside, state-of-the-art technology appealed to every geek.

I exited the car to let Champ stretch his legs. Well, that was my excuse. I figured the celebrity dog at my side, dressed for success in his logoed baseball cap, could only help my case. What else would encourage an impressionable teenager to spend time with me?

The celebrity bat dog caused an even bigger spectacle than I'd planned. The crush of mini-skirted coeds drama-posing with the black Lab almost caused Ella to bolt.

Dressed in comfy jeans, a sweatshirt with a silhouette of a rock-climber on the front, and her long, strawberry-kissed hair pulled back in a no-nonsense ponytail, Ella Sugarland epitomized nonconformity in a sea of girls trying too hard. Her sleek, wire-rimmed glasses and pressed-lip annoyance made her look Poindexter-smart too.

Before Ella could blow both of us off, Champ maneuvered out of the pack. He walked right to the girl's side and offered her his paw, elevating her to Miss Popularity, much to her irritation. Good thing the dog's antics melted her heart, or I think she would've walked the three miles to the stadium rather than getting into my vehicle.

"That sucked," Ella announced from the back seat. She sat cross-legged in the corner passenger side. I could see the designer tears in her jeans' knees in the rearview mirror since she'd insisted the dog sit up front with me.

"You're comfortable sitting like that?" My knees ached looking at the angles.

"Yeah. I think better when I sit like this."

I bit back a comment. "I'm sorry. I had no idea Champ would cause a riot." Actually, I had. I'd misjudged her reaction. I needed to learn how to charm teenagers.

Peacekeeper that he was, Champ poked his head around the seat toward Ella. She reached to scratch his ears. "He's super-cute. I wanted to meet him."

"Just not like this," I said.

"Ditto that." Her silence stretched between us.

"Champ is well-behaved but still has his dog moments. He stole the meat off my sandwich this afternoon." My stomach growled to prove it.

Ella's head popped between the seats as she continued to rub Champ's ears. "Bacon wasn't safe around my dad's dog either."

Visions of me fending off dogs at every meal came to mind.

Ella retreated to her corner of the back seat, her cell phone in hand.

Yikes. Beat by who knew what internet distraction? Not going to happen. I was more interesting. I just had to prove it to Ella. The question was, how did I start a conversation with a teenager? Just because I'd once been that hormone-ravaged, hot-mess young woman didn't mean I could communicate with another one twenty years later. What was I thinking, wanting children? They all grew into teenagers someday.

"Aunt Char told me you're a baseball fan." Not that I was, but establishing common ground required concessions.

"Duh. You're taking me to the stadium." Her eyes never left her phone.

No help there. "Aunt Char also said I would like you." She hadn't exactly said that, but desperation required small leaps of faith.

It worked. Ella looked up from her screen. "She said you could help me."

Thank you, Aunt Char. "How?"

"You're a reporter. Well, not so much anymore, but you were. I'm a reporter too."

"For the *Pack*." It wasn't a question. I'd read enough articles from Barkview High's newspaper for journalism contests over the years to know about the paper. I had no recollection of judging an entry from Ella, though. I'd bet her research skills were top-notch.

"Yeah. The story you did on Skye Barklay slaps. She bought my Nana Dolce's tequila caramels for the speakeasy."

Interesting. Ella had just given me a way in. "I didn't know that. That's a great addition to Skye's story." I met her eyes in the mirror. "Would you write it?"

"Me?" she squeaked, withdrawing again.

Was that shyness, or something else? "Yes. We can work together on it. The National Aviation Hall of Fame will love the

44

details." Everyone loved finding new links to Barkview's history. Me, especially. "We can discuss it over ice cream."

She went from engaged smile to crossed arms in no time. I'd stepped into something, for sure. "Why not? Don't you like ice cream?" Who didn't like ice cream?

"Nope."

Her emphatic "Nope" indicated more than dislike. Talk about censure. Was it something medical? "Are you lactose-intolerant?"

"No." Ella's hand brushed her waist, and I knew. In fact, a lot of things made sense now. Investigating Howard Looc's murder earlier last year had introduced me to the world of diabetes and a Bichon Frise.

"Was your dad a diabetic too?" I made a mental note to have Sandy look into his death.

"H-how'd you know?" I had her attention again.

"I solved a murder case that involved a Type I diabetic."

"My father told me about an invention that could change our lives."

If Howard had lived, maybe sooner rather than later. "Someday." An heiress to a candy company a diabetic? Clearly the gene ran in the family. Could spiking insulin levels explain Clark's personality swings too?

"What do you do at the stadium?" I asked. The team was practicing. No admissions.

"Work."

More one-word answers. Why she retreated puzzled me. "Ella…"

"I do the batting stats for Coach," she replied.

"Wow! That's impressive." I meant it.

"My dad taught me ERA percentages based on pitch selection. I can accurately predict pitch selection eighty percent of the time."

No clue what that meant, but... "Your dad would be proud of you."

I saw her flush in the rearview mirror. "Mom says I'm lame."

Her runway-perfect, yoga-sculpted mom. "She's wrong." A teenager more interested in using her brain than chasing boys? Had to love that. "It's good to remember your dad."

"Sometimes I can't remember exactly what he looked like."

Her admission touched me. Circumstance made us sisters. Big and little sisters. "You always will. I promise. I lost my dad too. I was angry for a long time. Mostly at my mom. She remarried too." Way too soon, I'd thought back then, but age does offer perspective.

"Your stepsister is fourteen years younger than you, isn't she?" Ella asked.

"Yes."

"My little brother's a terror. I have to watch him all the time."

"He is two," I pointed out. "I know you won't believe me, but it gets better."

"Right." Ella shook her head. I wouldn't have believed me either at her age.

"Why did you want to meet me today?" Ella asked.

Best to be direct. She seemed to appreciate that. "I wanted to know about the Candy Catcher baseball card."

Ella stiffened but, this time, didn't retreat. "Why? Has something happened to it?"

I hated to lie, but I couldn't tell her. Not yet. "I'm interested in knowing if it's possible that the other original cards were also saved."

"How would I know?" Another spark of interest.

"Your grandmother's papers might have a clue."

Ella chewed her lip. "You want to see them?"

"If you haven't read them, we can read them together."

"Grandma K said I had my whole life to read them."

"She's right." My intuition alerted me. What secrets did those papers contain—things a young girl shouldn't have to know about yet, or something else entirely?

"You really think the other cards survived?" No hiding Ella's interest in a lost treasure.

"I don't know. My reporter's mind is having a hard time accepting that only one survived."

I'd phrased that correctly. Ella considered my words before responding. "They'd be worth a lot of money. Grandma K said those cards were special. She wanted the Candy Catcher card displayed for everyone to admire."

"She was right. The baseball cards also tell the story of postwar Barkview."

Ella's reply was scornful. "I saw *Grease* and *Back to the Future*. The 1950s were about poodle skirts, leather jackets, and soda fountains."

"There was also McCarthyism and fear of nuclear war," I added. Innocence, yes, but the start of a major cultural shift.

"K."

"K what?" I hated Gen Z abbreviations.

"I'll bring my safety deposit key tomorrow. We can get the papers from the bank tomorrow after school."

My phone alarm went off: thirty minutes until Champ's next appearance. Much as my curiosity demanded Ella drop everything now, one of us had to be responsible. I had a bad feeling she'd win that contest. "Deal. I'll pick you up at the same place and time tomorrow?"

Ella scooted to the edge of the seat and scratched Champ's ears. "Leave Champ in the car."

"Sure." For a girl who didn't like attention, she had an adventurer's spirit. Be careful what you ask for, I reminded myself. Secrets were such for a reason. What secrets would Grandma K deem unworthy of her nephew Clark's scrutiny? Something about him or the family?

I dropped Ella at the stadium's north entrance, where thirty parked vehicles clustered around the players' entrance. Woofman's van was there too. Replacing the foul ball window just in time for the next slugger's shot seemed shortsighted, but who was I to question baseball's many traditions?

CHAPTER 6

Champ fetched the first stick for the Bonfire Beach Bash and added it to the enormous blaze with no help from me. In fact, other than chauffeuring him, I had no purpose. Once I stretched the blue jersey over his ears, the dog transformed into a focused working machine. He stood for all his selfies and paw-o-graphs with his goofy doggy smile no matter how the mob reacted.

I, on the other hand, lost patience early. Not that I didn't sympathize with the autograph seekers, but my need to solve the missing baseball card caper trumped photo ops.

Too bad karma didn't agree. I found Officer Casey Ann leaning over my windshield as Champ and I approached my illegally parked car. Furballs! Talk about bad luck. In my haste to get Champ to his appearance on time, I'd left my SUV in a loading zone. This ticket would cost me dearly for sure. It wasn't my first offense. Even I had to admit being caught parking illegally twice in one day had to be a record.

Recently promoted from midnight dispatch to traffic control, Casey Ann tended to do things by the book.

"I'm sorry. I was late for Champ's appearance and couldn't find a place to park." I gestured toward the dog, who must've sensed my distress and rubbed against my leg.

Was Casey Ann's smile understanding, or was it wishful thinking on my part? When she opened my passenger door and invited Champ inside, hope soared. "VIP duty isn't as easy as it looks." She handed me the familiar rectangular paper and grinned.

The words *Champ's Parking Pass* caused me to smile too.

"Careful. Next time I won't be as understanding."

"Thank you." I meant it. I offered her a Champ baseball card.

Casey Ann accepted the card, tapped her hat and waved me on. That I'd escaped another ticket made me wonder how much karma I had left.

I drove east on Pine Street to Fifth and parked beside Russ's SUV at police headquarters. With Champ at my side, I walked across the street to the Sit and Stay Café. No way I could arrive without bribery burgers for the chief and Russ at dinnertime.

Located on the corner of Fifth Street and Oak, the café occupied a quaint, green-gabled Craftsman bungalow built in 1921. Cheerful daffodils and colorful tulips overflowed from the hanging baskets swaying in the afternoon breeze on the spindle porch.

Dressed in Barkview Barkers jerseys and caps, some in the current blue-and-white-striped color scheme and others in the vintage white with sky-blue accents, the many veranda diners and their canine companions showed their team spirit. Champ fit in perfectly, strutting up the stone path like Caesar. What a ham.

I readied Champ's baseball cards for an impromptu meet and greet. But then Officer Richie Richards rushed out the green front door, the napkin protecting his uniform's shirtfront still tucked in his collar. His breathless "Excuse me" as he jogged by me spurred speculation that changed the café's air of excitement to concern. It was made even worse when Nell, the café's owner, filled the doorway, holding Richie's forgotten doggie bag. Wisps escaped her neat chignon, a testament to her haste. The burger burglar Richie Richards leave dinner behind? Only serious police business could interfere with his consumption of grilled sirloin and onions.

My mouth watered at the wafting aroma. Forget my usual chicken salad order tonight. A burger smelled too good to say no to.

"What's going on?" I asked.

"I have no idea. He was having dinner with his cousin. Next thing I knew, he ran out the door." Like her patrons, Nell had also dressed in a blue-and-white-striped jersey and a Barkers baseball scarf that accented her dark good looks.

"His cousin?" I asked.

"That's how he introduced him." Nell pivoted to her right and pointed toward a lone man at the corner table. Although this stranger was dark-haired and leaner, there was no missing the family resemblance in his square jaw and blue eyes. "His name is Hunter Richards. He's in town with the baseball card convention."

"What does he do?" I asked.

"He's a memorabilia dealer," Nell explained.

"How many dealers are there?"

"A lot." Nell chuckled. "Don't tell Hunter he's not our one and only. I think he could sell ice in Siberia."

Her amusement got my attention. "Interested in him?"

"Naw. He's a Jack Russell kind of guy. Sandy might like him," Nell admitted.

Only in Barkview could that single reference say so much.

That Nell had taken the time to consider it meant something too. Maybe my friend was ready to consider a relationship.

My twenty questions never got asked. Blur, Nell's lovable black Labrador Retriever, practically tripped Nell as she squeezed through her legs to direct-sniff Champ. No offense taken. The bat dog returned Blur's welcome with an intimate sniff of his own.

So much for training. Blur's Hollywood-worthy come-hither look worked. Champ followed, jerking my arm in his haste. Naturally, two top-of-their-game athletic dogs would be interested in one another.

Nell must've seen it coming. She blocked Champ's path, allowing me recovery time. "Champ. Sit," I said. This romance was not going anywhere.

The dog's pout (yes, a pout) tugged at my sense of fairness. Sure, he deserved a break, but Michael would kill me if I let him go astray. I held my ground. "Champ. Sit."

The Lab sighed and obeyed, his accusatory look saying "Casanova-killer."

"Well done." Nell's praise meant a lot. We'd been through too many you-need-a-dog discussions of late—the kind only really good friends can get away with.

Before I could thank her and place my order, two police cars squealed out of the station's parking lot, lights flashing, and headed south on Fifth Street.

The stadium wasn't the only building in that direction, I reminded myself. My pounding heart wasn't buying it. A full minute later, Russ's text confirmed my fears.

Ella is okay. She's shook up. Someone tried to break into the stadium. Meet us here as soon as you can. Ella's asking for you. Haven't found her mother or connected with your aunt yet.

"OMG!" I covered my mouth too late. I felt every eye in the place on me. Panic did that to me as possibilities crowded my head. What wasn't Russ telling me? Could this have been an attempted abduction? Had my interest in the girl somehow caused it? It didn't take a doctoral degree to figure out what I wanted from Ella.

Nell gestured for me to follow her toward the sidewalk, away from unwanted eavesdropping. "What's happening?"

"Russ says Ella caught someone breaking into the stadium," I replied.

"Was Ella the target?" Nell asked.

"No. Russ didn't say that..." Was there more to it than a simple break in? "I can't believe this is happening. I picked her up from school only a few hours ago."

"I know," Nell replied softly.

The moment Ella had gotten into my car, Barkview's gossip network had started speculating.

"Did your aunt ask you to pick her up?" Nell asked.

Not exactly the truth, but it was the answer that would protect Ella best. I still couldn't lie to Nell. "No. I wanted to know about the Candy Catcher's baseball card. Ella said we could get Grandma K's original bequest from the family box tomorrow."

"It's possible someone tried to grab her to stop you from seeing Grandma K's files." Nell chewed the inside of her cheek. "You need to see RJ Ruff."

The owner of the local sports memorabilia shop? Once upon a time, he'd rented a storefront. A casualty of online shopping, he now rented a small industrial warehouse in the Barkview Industrial Complex. "Why?"

Nell's foot-to-foot weight shift bothered me. "There's been talk about a series of baseball cards coming to auction."

"So? Baseball cards are traded daily." Someone needed to explain the adult fascination with children's trading cards and the crazy valuations.

"Rumor has it it's the Fab Five set."

Talk about a bomb. "How is that even possible? Legally, the Candy Catcher card belongs to Ella and is loaned to Barkview's baseball card museum for ten years."

"I'm sure there's an opt-out clause of some sort," Nell said. "For security or attendance?"

An interesting point. Had the card's theft activated one of those clauses? Concern danced in my stomach. "The card is too well known to be sold on the black market."

"Clear provenance isn't always a deal breaker." Nell looked everywhere but at me. Had she acquired something on the sly?

"The law calls that stolen property." And too many other things to list. Who was this person who looked like my too-honest friend? "How do you know about this?" I wasn't going to like the answer, I could tell by her pained expression.

"I'm a-a collector."

"You!" We'd have a long talk about this someday.

She seemed hurt. "I told you my grandfather left my sister and me the family's baseball card collection." In addition to the building, the café, and the dog treat company run by Nell's sister Melanie (Mel for short). "You said it was boxes of dusty, well-used trading cards."

"I was wrong. Mel sorted them and found a 1952 Topps Mickey Mantle rookie card worth close to $1 million."

My turn to stare. "You can't be serious."

"The same card in 9.5+ shape sold for $12 million. I can't believe it either." I hardly recognized the awe in her voice.

"Hope you have that card locked up safely." What else could I say? I didn't get it.

"I do. Just imagine what the complete Fab Five card set would be worth."

I couldn't. "The complete set is pure speculation."

"Is it?" A scary treasure-hunter fever burned in Nell's dark eyes. "How could only one card survive? It makes no sense. Ella is the key to finding the rest of them."

Nell, the voice of reason, the most rational business owner I'd ever met, losing it over baseball cards? I'd never have believed it.

No controlling the shiver that shot the length of my spine, I crossed my arms in an attempt to hide it. "Should I have Uncle G question you?"

Her short laugh returned us both to normalcy. "No way. I'm just passing on what I heard. That poor child has been through enough."

I agreed. Caution still tempered my next move. Fortune-hunting turned regular people into obsessives. Protecting Barkview's history was a full-time job.

I placed the dinner order for delivery to the stadium. Never underestimate a stress eater, either. I ordered a burger for me too.

Champ and I trotted back to my car. I drove like an Indy racer to the stadium to make up the five-minute delay I'd taken at Nell's. Uncle G's SUV with K-9 tags, two police SUVs, Russ's Land Rover, and a handful of black SUVs from Blue Diamond Security, Russ's company, clustered around the players-only entrance. Otherwise, nothing had changed in the two hours since I'd last been here.

I chose a legal parking spot, but the open loading curb did tease my good sense. Then I followed the Barker VIP signs to the turnstile entrance where a Barkers Baseball security guard met us.

"The chief's waiting for you in the coach's box. Second floor, then go left toward home plate." He scratched Champ's ears. The dog rotated his head, offering a better angle.

I handed the man a signed baseball card. "I'll find him." Inside, Champ pulled me toward the stairs, but I redirected him toward the elevator. No way I'd be out of breath entering Uncle G's military-police-style interrogation.

The chief met me the moment the elevator doors opened. Flanked by his pair of iron-gray German Shepherds that matched his neatly clipped beard and full head of hair, he looked enough like his dogs to reconfirm my canine-master look alike theory. His navy-blue shirt with silver epaulettes coordinated with the dogs' police vests.

I wrapped Champ's leash around my hand for no reason. The Lab handled the Shepherd intimidation with his usual laid-back ease. A shared sniff and everything was okay until my tall, dark, and insanely handsome husband leaned toward me for a kiss. Not on Champ's watch. In a flash of black fur, the dog wiggled between us and barked. Not once, but repeatedly until Russ stepped back.

Shocked, I could only stare. What happened to the mellow dog who let every fan pet and scratch him?

"Champ." I swear Russ's no-nonsense tone drew the dog's glare. Russ offered his hand for a friendly sniff and then reached for mine and squeezed it. "We'll share."

I stumbled as the Lab pressed his full weight against my thigh, staking his own claim. Russ steadied me.

Not another testosterone thing. I sputtered, "There's enough of me for both of you." Me, bond with another dog? I hadn't believed it the first time, either. G-paw, the fun-loving Golden Doodle who'd helped me solve the Skye Barklay case, had connected with me too. This situation was different. Champ would be home with his owner in a few days—not that the dog knew it. He still relied on me. He had no one else.

I scratched the bat dog's head reassuringly and traced Russ's clean-shaven jaw with the other hand. "We all need to get along."

No missing the mutual size-up.

"Fight it out at another time." Uncle G's booming voice drew everyone's attention, including Champ's. "Ella needs all our focus now."

His levity worked. Both males shook it off. We all followed the chief through the VIP lounge. The way the leather and reclining chairs were grouped into intimate sitting areas reminded me more of a comfy living room than a sports facility.

Suddenly, Champ jerked forward, ripping the leash from my hand. He darted through the door separating the lounge from the glassed-in staff observation area. Inside, the wall hangings celebrated past pennant glory, and eight desks lined the window. With unobstructed views of the field and both teams' dugouts, those desks would allow anyone sitting there to see it all.

Champ huddled with Ella on the floor. That her thin arms wrapped around him as if he were a lifesaver once again proved the dog's sixth sense regarding human trauma.

Ella's troubled gaze about tore me apart. Champ scooted aside as I eased my creaky knee down until I could kneel beside her. "What happened?"

"I was sitting on the floor." Her gulp-sniffle combination betrayed her fear. "I saw someone come out of the stairwell. I got up and asked them what they were doing..."

I hugged her tighter. "That was really brave." More courage than sense. I could relate. So could Russ if his tight jaw could be called agreement.

"He wore a President Reagan mask."

"You recognized the president?" Reagan had passed before Ella had been born. Either Barkview High was doing a great job educating, or...

"I saw *Point Break*," Ella explained. "I didn't recognize the man."

Another reference to classic movies. She must be a fan.

"How did you know it was a man?" Uncle G asked.

"He was built like a man. Kinda stocky, with wide shoulders."

I understood that. I stopped Uncle G's request for clarification. "Anything else recognizable about him?"

Ella glanced at the ceiling and gnawed at her lower lip. "Reagan kinda seemed familiar, but maybe it's because Mom watches his black-and-white movies all the time."

"What was familiar about him?" Uncle G barking with full investigative vigor intimidated better than a giant.

Even I recoiled from his fervor. Russ stepped in and waved off the chief, who thankfully understood good-cop-bad-cop techniques and retreated.

Russ knelt beside us both, his tablet ready. "Did he wear gloves?" he asked calmly.

I could've kissed him. Ella kept talking.

"Black. He carried a black backpack over his shoulder," Ella replied without hesitation.

"Was he wearing jeans?" I asked. Ella's keen observation skills made her a good witness.

She closed her eyes. "Black jogging pants. The shoes weren't regular tennies."

"What do you mean?" I asked.

"My stepdad has twenty pairs of court shoes. These were higher around the ankle."

"Like hiking boots?" Russ suggested.

Ella nodded.

"How did you get away?" I knew I'd be impressed, and she didn't disappoint me.

"I ran in here and locked the door when I saw the mask." She bit her lip. Champ licked her hand. "I pulled my Hootie."

"What's that?" I asked. This Gen Z vocabulary was killing me.

Ella pointed to the inch-long tube on her backpack. "It's a screech alarm. The Hootie's really loud. My dad gave it to me. He told me if anyone ever bothers me to pull it and scream. I did and waved at the field. Coach saw me."

Talk about a clear head. I whispered, "Your dad was watching out for you."

"You think so?" The sudden light in her eyes reassured me. She'd be okay. Ella Sugarland defined survivor.

"I know so," I said.

"Where'd the masked man go?" Uncle G asked.

"He saw me and I ran." Ella shuddered. "He went back into the stairwell."

Uncle G's intimidating frown didn't seem appropriate. Before I could take issue, Keke Sugarland-Russo sailed into the room.

Clad in chic yoga leggings, a crop top that accented her sculpted body, and dangling diamond earrings that glittered in her flowing dark hair, she looked more like a Lululemon catalog ad than a mother of a teenager. "Darling. Oh, darling."

Ella tensed. "Save me."

Her plea stirred my protective instincts. Champ's too. I'd just met Ella, but even I knew spectacle caused her to withdraw. A tearful mother still trumped my position. The bat dog and I retreated.

The ensuing Kardashian-style melodrama confirmed that my mom and I had no issues. I even pitied Justin Russo, the hot-shot tennis pro with the six-pack to solidify his qualifications, married to this drama queen.

I scooted to Russ's side across the room while Champ tossed his head and nosed his way to Ella's Barkers Baseball backpack tucked in the corner by the door. He sniffed all around the tile floor and returned to my side, poking his nose into my hip. I ignored him.

"Why doesn't Uncle G believe Ella?" I asked.

Russ denied nothing. "The man did not escape down the stairwell. No one entered or exited the downstairs door into the lobby during the time frame."

Ella lying? I didn't believe it. "The security guard could've stepped away."

"The cameras concur."

"I didn't know they had cameras here." Surveillance security in Barkview? Times were changing.

"Only the GM and the techs on my team know," Russ replied. "The footage does not appear to have been altered."

At least he'd considered the possibility. "You don't think Ella lied either, do you?"

He neither agreed nor disagreed. He'd seen the girl's ready-to-bolt look. There was no way he believed that she'd want that over-the-top attention.

Champ tossed his head and poked my hip again. I pointed to the ground. He obeyed with an exaggerated exhale.

Uncle G heard it too. "You drove Ella to the stadium today." It wasn't really a question or an accusation. Just a statement.

I answered anyway. "Yes. I wanted to talk to her about the Candy Catcher baseball card. She offered to give me Grandma K's notes on the card. Could I have caused this?" My voice cracked. I couldn't verbalize my fears.

"We don't know anything yet." Uncle G's reply didn't help.

Russ's shoulder touch did. "None of this is your fault. If the masked man was in here, they know something about this stadium that we do not."

His assurances helped. "Could they have gone to the roof instead of the ground floor?"

Uncle G's clenched teeth answered that one. He'd checked. "They couldn't have disappeared into thin air."

"Could they have been looking for something else? What else is on this floor?" I asked.

"The field suites are all empty. There's a sales office, and the GM's office down the third base hall," Russ said.

"Nothing valuable in the GM's office?"

Uncle G referred to his notes. "A couple of signed memorabilia items. Petty cash is under five hundred dollars. Robbery seems unlikely."

Which left us with Ella being the target. It just felt wrong. "Could a potential kidnapper seriously be so inept?"

Uncle G's toothpick spun a full revolution. "Few criminals are intelligent."

If not Ella, they must've wanted something. I sucked in my breath at the same time Champ bumped my thigh so hard I stumbled. Russ caught me before I landed on my face. What was wrong with the dog?

"What's in your pocket?" Uncle G asked.

"Nothing..." I patted the pocket and removed a few of Champ's signed baseball cards. "It's..." The Lab headbutted my hand. The cards fluttered to the ground. The dog circled them. What?

"Champ, fetch," Uncle G ordered.

The black Lab looked from the chief to me and back again, his body vibrating with energy. "The command is, 'Champ, bring it back,'" I announced.

Like a competitive sprinter clearing the blocks, the Lab sprang for the door, his blue nylon leash clicking as it bounced across the tile floor. Uncle G's hand command sent the German Shepherds in pursuit.

Champ skidded to a halt at the stairwell door and barked.

Once, twice...he kept going until Uncle G opened the door. The black Lab darted down the stairs.

Weapon ready, Uncle G ordered me, "Stay here," and disappeared with Russ and the German Shepherd deputies right behind.

Not a chance. I practically held my breath as I trailed behind, cautiously watching. Champ had detoured toward the stairs on arrival. He'd sensed something then, and I'd missed it.

The bat dog's overexcited barking echoed in the concrete stairwell. My head didn't pound this time. My heart did. He'd found something.

CHAPTER 7

The faint line between the bottom of the concrete wall and floor would've been missed without Champ pawing at the wall. Pocketknife in hand, Russ scraped away enough concrete to confirm that the line was not a natural crack.

"There's a secret door." It was the only possible explanation. Why else would the dog be so focused on it?

No missing Uncle G's eye roll. Call it winning-lotto kind of luck, but even I knew that dogs sensed things. "How else do you explain the man Ella saw just disappearing?" I added.

The chief's growl almost concurred.

"What's on the other side of the wall?" I asked.

Amanda's familiar voice from the top stairwell step sounded surreal. "The Fab Five display." Although her attire hadn't changed since this morning, her crumpled blouse and stained slacks told exactly what kind of day she'd had. "I heard scratching against the wall and came to investigate. The guard told me what happened. There were rumors about a secret door years ago. We even looked for it during the remodel. We never found a secret door, just a closed-off storage closet. In the end, I assumed the secret room was nothing more than an old wives' tale."

Notebook ready, Uncle G asked, "Who was in the museum an hour ago?"

Amanda patted her hair. "I don't know. I docented a youth baseball card collectors' club tour. No one manned the museum's front doors for forty-five minutes."

"Anyone could've entered and left without you seeing them," I said.

Russ was right. My contact with Ella hadn't caused this. "Where was Stallone?" Surely, no one could sneak by Amanda's Bassett Hound.

"Napping in the entryway sun." She smiled. "He's my best receptionist. He barks when someone walks by him."

"Unless he knew them," Uncle G added.

I scribbled on a Post-it and stuffed it into my pocket. That limited the suspects to frequent visitors and Barkview residents. "Who organized today's tour?"

"RJ Ruff."

Nell's warning about the man made this second reference doubly important. "He sells sports memorabilia that he distributes from Barkview," I said for Russ's benefit.

"He hosts these introductions to baseball events often," Amanda added. "He's a big contributor to youth sports programs. He pays the kids' entry fees and supplies their teams with needed equipment. You should see him with the kids. He's great."

Amanda was a fan. Ruff sounded just like the man who'd bought the old Sugarland home down the road from me.

"How many chaperones were on the tour?" Russ asked.

"Five. The bus driver also joined us," Amanda replied.

I'd check in with RJ Ruff myself. Right now, the secret room interested me. "Tell me more about the rumor of the secret room. When and why was there one?"

"Not much to tell. It supposedly connected to the home team's locker room and was used for assignations."

"Why would anyone want to go to a smelly boys' locker room?" I blushed as my words tumbled out. If I hadn't known, Russ's suggestive look would've spelled it out. The better question was, what teenager wouldn't want a private room, no matter what it smelled like?

"You did find the secret, uh, assignation room," Uncle G said.

"Maybe. We found a storage space of sorts on the other side of this wall. It didn't have a welcome note. We removed the wall to make room for the Fab Five display."

"What does that mean?" I asked.

"It was just empty space between the walls with no access," Amanda replied. "It was likely a walled closet."

I focused on the concrete wall with just that single hairline crack. Finding the last tunnel hadn't been easy either, I reminded myself. That door had been part of rumrunner tunnels that crisscrossed the north side of town. A precocious Golden Doodle and I had found them while trying to clear Skye Barklay of murder charges.

In this case, exactly how the door operated didn't matter as much as where it went and who knew about it, I reminded myself. Still, I couldn't shake the memory of the subterranean earthquake. Champ's warm body pressed against my side, oddly comforting. Somehow, he knew my fears and had my back.

I scratched his ears. "Why is the Fab Five's display located where it is?" I asked. That the museum's most popular display had been shoved into a corner had always seemed odd to me.

"Grandma K wanted it there and designed the other

displays around it," Amanda replied. "I heard that the original design was written on a napkin," she added. "It was PA. That's pre-Amanda."

My heart pounded. "A napkin?" That hardly seemed like Grandma K's style. "Do you know where that napkin is?"

"I would guess in Grandma K's papers," Amanda said. "I asked her for it for the museum's archives, but she refused. Said it was a family matter."

It sounded like a piece of Barkview history to me. Another reference to Grandma K's private papers couldn't be a coincidence. Russ and I shared a glance with Uncle G. There was way more going on here than a stolen baseball card. "If something happens to Ella, who inherits the family papers?" I asked.

Uncle G shook his head. "If Ella hasn't designated an heir, her mother would need to petition the court for access."

A fifteen-year-old have a will? Most adults didn't. Russ spoke before I could verbalize the obvious. "We have some digging to do."

I got his hint. Time to get Sandy and Jennifer's exceptional computer skills involved. I checked my watch. If I hurried, I'd catch Sandy right before my aunt's show went live.

Champ's stomach growl changed that plan. My husband touched my shoulder. "Looks like Champ's hungry."

I was too.

Russ's whisper was for my ears only. "I'll be here awhile. Champ's had a rough day. Take him home, feed him, and let him run in the yard."

I nodded. How my husband knew so much about dogs still surprised me. He walked Champ and me to the car and kissed me goodbye. I dialed Sandy as I turned up the winding road toward the Terraces. Thirty minutes until my aunt's showtime wasn't exactly the best timing, but...

"Hey, Boss. Ella okay?" Sandy's upbeat, nothing-can't-be-fixed tone impressed me. She'd taken to the executive producer's position well.

I pictured the Star Trek–inspired control panel in the phone booth we fondly called our studio control room snow-capped with her notes. While I preferred multicolored Post-its, Sandy liked simple cues. After all the years she'd chided my visual aids as dinosaurish, she'd opted for the same noncomputerized reminders.

"Keke has taken her home." I wouldn't comment on Ella's happiness, but she was at least physically safe with her mother. "I'm taking Champ home. Can you join us after the show?"

"Sure. Conference time?"

"I will stop by too." Aunt Char's distant voice saved me another call. Her relationship with Ella made her input important as well.

"Perfect. I'll text Jennifer too," I said. Barkview's former librarian turned KDOG general manager was the best researcher around. And it looked like we needed one now.

Jennifer confirmed she'd be there as I opened my garage door. I drove inside, not stopping until a bright yellow pickleball hanging on a string rested on my windshield. The bumper dent in the gray fiberboard cabinets lining the garage made this parking crutch a win for everyone.

Champ sat at attention on the passenger seat beside me, his nose airborne as he sniffed in multiple directions. When he placed his paw on my hand as I unclipped my seatbelt, I saw the questioning look in his dark eyes. My heart melted. The poor dog had been ripped from the familiar and placed in my untutored care. I scratched his head. "It'll be okay, boy. This is my house. You're safe here."

He rubbed his head against my shoulder, sending a puff of black hair everywhere. So much for Labs not shedding much.

Stress shedding had taken over, not that I blamed him. Russ's allergies were another story. Guilt stirred. No way I could leave Champ outside. Russ would need to take his allergy meds until Champ left.

The Lab's gaze never left me as I walked around the car to the passenger door to let him out. The dog jumped to the ground and stuck by my side as I unloaded his travel bag and cooler from the back. The massive dog bed would have to wait for Russ. Not that it appeared particularly heavy, but the awkward shape made door navigation a job for my husband.

I braced myself as I deactivated the alarm. My last dog visitors, the Dachshunds, had just about tripped me in their haste to get inside the house. Champ, in contrast, remained practically glued to my side, despite his wild sniffing. Had to love this well-trained dog.

Together we walked through the butler's pantry and into the kitchen. Lined with plantation-style cabinets topped with glass displays showcasing Russ and my many vineyard adventures, the kitchen invited friends to gather around a large, flecked granite center island.

I placed Champ's bags on the counter and unclipped his leash. My house may not be exactly dog-friendly, but I doubted the Lab would get into trouble. In fact, after a sniff around the room, he seemed more interested in his cooler on the counter than further exploration. My stomach growled in confirmation.

I dug two silver bowls from Champ's travel duffle, filled one with water, placed it on the floor, and opened the cooler. Beneath the gel packs I discovered six bags of The Farmer's Dog food with Champ's name on the label. Light brown in color, with chunks of orange that I assumed were carrots and green bits of something I couldn't identify, the pricey fresh food reminded me of the product provided by our many

Barkview barkeries. It still looked and smelled like vomit to me, but what did I know?

Champ liked it or, I daresay, loved it based on his anticipatory panting as I cut open the bag and squeezed it into his bowl. I placed it on the floor, but Champ didn't dig in. He just sat there licking his lips, his front feet vibrating, and looking at me with beseeching eyes. He was waiting for a command.

The realization hit me hard. Like Gem, the well-trained German Shepherd I'd dog-sat for, Champ wouldn't eat without permission. The curse of a well-trained dog. He could starve if I didn't find the right words.

Panic set in as I fumbled through my shoulder bag, looking for the short list of commands Sandy had given to me. I found the crumpled page lined with familiar print: *Sit. Down. Off. Drop it. Heel. Go.* Nothing about eating. Of course.

My eyes met Champ's. "Okay."

Champ's nose dove into the bowl. I'd guessed it. Or maybe he just wanted to eat. I didn't care which. Talk about stress. I went right to the wine cooler on the bar and poured a generous glass of shiraz-du-jour. With nothing but condiments in the cupboards and basics on the fridge shelves, a whatever-is-available quesadilla would have to do.

Champ cleaned his bowl, policed around it, and then beelined to the French doors before I'd even turned on the skillet. He needed to go out, I realized, and I hurried through the great room to open the door. The dog took off across the travertine patio toward the pickleball court, circled it, and did a lap around the grass before returning to my feet, tongue out and panting—the same look he had when fetching a baseball bat.

So much for my hot dinner. I went back inside for a ball I'd seen in Champ's duffle and grabbed a handful of peanut butter pretzels. With protein, carbs, and fat, they met the well-balanced meal criteria.

Jennifer found me on my hands and knees with my head under a bougainvillea about twenty minutes later. Champ's bark had warned me she'd arrived, but I couldn't give up the hunt.

"What are you looking for?" Dressed in jeans and a vintage Barkers Baseball sweatshirt that set off her dark eyes, Jennifer looked casual yet elegant with her tawny hair twisted into a messy bun.

I backed out from beneath the shrub and stood. "A ball. Apparently, my fetch game needs work." And my hunting skills. I'd been so sure the missing ball had ricocheted here.

Champ nosed past me. He rustled around and backed out with the ball in his mouth. I really was blind. Instead of dropping the ball at my feet for another throw, he stood in front of Jennifer, blinking.

My attention focused on the wine glass she dangled in front of my eyes.

"I figured you'd need this." Jennifer handed me the glass and picked a leaf from my hair.

I shook my head, dropping even more plant debris. Ugh! "Thanks. I'll go over everything when Sandy and Aunt Char get here. Right now, I need to know everything you can find out about a secret door in Barker Stadium."

She chuckled. "There's been a rumor of one for years, but no record of ever finding it." She paused. I could see her librarian hat falling into place. "You found it, didn't you?"

Jennifer whipped a laptop out of the tote slung over her shoulder just as Champ sniffed her. "He smells Cinnamon and Nutmeg." Jennifer held out her hand. "It's okay, boy."

The Lab agreed. He leaned in for a head scratch that Jennifer gladly performed.

"Why didn't you bring your dogs?" Jennifer rarely went anywhere without her twin ruby Cavaliers.

"It's after their bedtime."

Enough said. Messing with a Cavalier's schedule rarely turned out well.

"Why are you interested in this hypothetical door?" Jennifer asked.

I motioned her to follow me into the great room. "I think it has something to do with the Fab Five."

"Superstars," she huffed. "If not for baseball, those five boys would've been in juvenile hall." She sat on the leather sectional and set her computer on the coffee table. Had to love the way her fingers flew across the keyboard.

"You're not being too critical, are you?" I asked. Jennifer had no patience for hooliganism, as she called it.

"Hardly. Barkview remembers them as heroes. That was far from the truth, except maybe for Owen Daniels. The rest of the boys behaved like entitled troublemakers."

"Karl?"

"The worst of the lot. He and Bertie Wallace, uh, borrowed a police car for a beach cruise," Jennifer said.

A career-ending felony back then. What were they thinking? "Who fixed it?" Someone had. I'd never heard this story.

"The Fab Five's baseball coach. If he hadn't the two would've lost their shot at the pros. Back then, baseball was all apple pie and Chevrolet. No scandals allowed," Jennifer explained. "Where exactly is this secret door?"

"Amanda told me there was one behind the Fab Five display," I replied.

Jennifer scrolled through a document. "In 1952, the university team played at the current stadium." She uploaded a drawing onto her screen. "Interesting. Before the renovation, the museum space would've been part of the home team's locker room."

My intuition went on full alert. I patted my pocket for a Post-it. Jennifer handed me a pad and pen to scribble a reminder. "Someone was sneaking someone or something in?"

"Or out," Jennifer agreed.

As with the Skye Barklay investigation, I realized answers would be found in the past. Barkview circa 1950, to be exact.

CHAPTER 8

Sandy, Aunt Char, and Renny arrived before Jennifer could dig deeper. After her usual room survey, the queen Cavalier permitted Champ a sniff—nothing intimate or too familiar, but at least friendly, leaving no doubt who ruled this situation. She then strolled to the great room and settled into her favorite spot in the center of the sofa. With a headshake, Champ took his cue and curled up on a soft fleece blanket Sandy had placed by the fireplace. I needed to take a page from his easygoing attitude. The dog sure had his priorities straight. No wonder he excelled at dealing with the public.

Dressed in the same navy Dior suit in which she'd presented Champ with the Bone to the City, Aunt Char still looked as fresh and unruffled as she'd looked at noon. Sandy also wore the same Barkers Baseball jersey. Was I the only one feeling like something the cat dragged in, still dressed in my yard-tarnished slacks?

"What you need to know before we start is that the Candy Catcher's baseball card has been stolen." No sense keeping that information from the team. I trusted them all. Besides, effectively making connections required all the facts.

My announcement surprised no one, except maybe Aunt Char, who seemed to choke on her champagne bubbles. "Aunt Char, are you okay?"

My aunt about collapsed on the sofa beside Renny. "I'm afraid the missing baseball card may be related to Ella's incident."

"Why is that?" I crossed my arms, not backing down until Aunt Char spoke.

She drew us all into a tight circle. "This is highly confidential." And clearly uncomfortable for an admission. "Canine Caramel is not financially sound."

"Everybody knows that. Gabby's been talking about it for weeks," Sandy said.

Aunt Char's instant relief indicated just how sensitive that information was.

"How bad?" I asked.

"Not unfixable," Aunt Char said. "Yet."

"For you. Can Clark fix it?" I asked.

Aunt Char shrugged. "I've suggested that he hire an excellent CFO. Clark and Jordan hold controlling interests in the candy company. Ella's minority position allows me to suggest only." That had to be frustrating. "If word gets out to his creditors, it could be catastrophic."

Which would adversely affect Ella as well. Was Clark foolish enough to ignore Aunt Char's considerable financial skills? "Is that why he would have wanted the Candy Catcher baseball card?"

"The sale would certainly have helped the balance sheet," Aunt Char admitted.

Grandma K asking Aunt Char to be her executor made perfect sense now. Aunt Char would protect Ella.

"Do you think Clark will hire the CFO?" Sandy asked.

"I am hopeful. He and his son are stubborn. We will know for sure sometime next week."

That it wasn't a sure thing bothered me for Ella's sake.

"Canine Caramel is a part of Barkview's past. Isn't there something we can do to help them?" Sandy asked.

"Times change. Businesses must adapt to remain relevant," Jennifer replied. "The city can't subsidize bad business decisions."

I agreed with that.

"The First Street store is a 1950s time capsule. It's a total tourist draw," Sandy insisted.

"Or a testament to Clark's aversion to change," Jennifer remarked. "The company still uses the clunky old Rose Forgrove wrapping machine to package their caramels."

Sandy whistled as she looked up from her tablet. "You're right. That's inefficient. The machine only wraps one hundred caramels a minute."

"That's bad?" It seemed like a lot of candy to me.

"Current twist-wrap machines will package three to five hundred per minute. That's five times the production," Sandy explained.

Visions of the iconic scene in *I Love Lucy* in which she tried to keep up with candy production came to mind. "Canine Caramel does short-batch caramels. Do they really need that kind of efficiency?"

"If they want to remain competitive, they do." Aunt Char's solemn comment confirmed Sandy's assessment. "The caramel apple portion of the business is doing well. It is a more labor-intensive product."

The gourmet apples coated with the company's famous caramel and decorated with chocolate, pretzels, candies, and other yummy confections were works of art.

"Canine Caramel hasn't measurably remodeled since the fire back in 1952," Jennifer said. "In fact, the company was in financial trouble back then too. Some say the fire saved the company since insurance money paid for the new building and equipment."

"The insurance money wasn't the entire solution. Barkview rallied behind them," Aunt Char added. "The city gave the Sugarlands an interest-free loan on the land in the industrial complex."

"Wow! Look at this." We all huddled around Sandy's tablet. Photos featuring slogans such as "Save Our Candy" and "For Sweet Victory" showed massive fundraisers. Karl had no choice but to quit baseball when his father passed. I, of all people, understood the pressure that responsibility brought.

"What caused the fire?" I asked. The world had changed for the better for Canine Caramel that day.

"The official cause was a fire in a caramel cooker. Then the sugar stored nearby ignited and caused explosions," Jennifer explained.

"I didn't know sugar was flammable." Did I need to worry about my pantry exploding?

"Granulated sugar isn't. Powdered sugar is. The heating vat was either left on or turned on by faulty electrical wires. It happened on a Sunday at 1 a.m. Fortunately, the building was empty, so no one was hurt." Jennifer paused before adding, "I'll head to the archives in the morning and look for the official report."

"I imagine the explosions caused traumatic episodes for the war veterans," Aunt Char said.

I hadn't thought of that. It must've sounded like bombs dropping. "From what Gabby tells me, it doesn't sound like Owen's injuries that night were caused by a car accident."

What did Aunt Char's sharp look mean? "I'd like to see Gabby's granny's report, if you don't mind."

I made a note to follow up with Gabby. "What are you thinking?"

"Canine Caramel is in a difficult place right now. I'd like to know the truth before accusations start flying."

I understood that. Was Canine Caramel's success their own or built on a past lie? "Does Ella know about her uncle's finances?"

Aunt Char shook her head. How like my aunt to protect the girl. "Over the past few months, there have been numerous offers to purchase the card. I turned them down at Ella's request."

"Why did Ella turn them down?" I had to ask, but I knew.

"Grandma K wanted the card to be enjoyed by all. Ella chose to honor her request."

Despite what had to have been eye-opening offers. Ella really was a remarkable young woman. "How many offers were there?"

"Three reasonable ones. One very generous."

"Clark had to be furious that he couldn't control the card's destiny." Aunt Char's exhale confirmed my words.

"Who wanted to buy them?" Jennifer asked the important question.

"I don't know," Aunt Char replied. "Mr. Ruff insisted that his buyers wished to remain anonymous. I understand the practice is common."

Another avenue leading to RJ Ruff and his mysterious collectors. I'd see him in the morning. Not that he'd share his clients' information. Tracking down those potential buyers wouldn't be easy. I glanced at Sandy, who was already typing madly on her tablet.

"I have something." That was fast, even for computer-savvy Sandy. "Mr. Ruff changed his name. His birth name was Rufus Jackson Ruff."

"Ruf Ruff?" Grade school had to have been a nightmare for him. Suddenly, being named after the California island I'd been conceived on didn't seem so bad. "His parents were evil."

"Ten years ago, he legally changed it to RJ Ruff. I followed his ancestry back to a minor Hollywood actress."

"Did RJ play ball?" I asked.

"No. It appears he made his money in import-export. Collecting became his contribution to the sport," Sandy replied.

Jennifer interjected, "RJ's maternal grandfather was a minister. Not sure how an Iowa minister's daughter made it to Hollywood, but I don't see a Fab Five connection."

"Barkview has certainly benefited from his generosity," Aunt Char said.

A dead end. "Have you seen Grandma K's private papers?" I asked.

"No."

I believed her. Although my aunt remained on the sofa, rhythmically stroking Renny's back, I sensed more.

"Do you have access to them?" I felt like a prosecutor dealing with an uncooperative witness.

"I do as the guardian of her estate." Was the tightness around Aunt Char's eyes exhaustion or concern? "I prefer to have Ella's permission. She's asked me to stop by her home tonight and pick up her key. I assume she will give it to me at that time. Apparently, her mother is refusing to let her leave the house tomorrow."

"That has to be making her day." My dry remark drew a smile from everyone except Aunt Char.

"I don't disagree with Keke," Aunt Char announced. "The

chief can't tell us if the intruder was after Ella or circumstance put at the wrong place at the wrong time."

"Champ potentially located a secret door from the stadium's entrance to the 1950s Barker locker room. It may have been the escape route for the man Ella saw," I added.

Aunt Char nodded. "I'm glad. Ella needs to be believed."

"I never doubted her."

Aunt Char smiled. "I will contact the bank in the morning. As much as I believe family secrets should remain such, we must do all we can to protect Ella." Renny jumped to the ground at the same time Aunt Char rose to leave. Their in-sync behavior amazed me sometimes. "Meet me at the Barkview Bank at 9 a.m."

Champ snored through Aunt Char's parting hugs and good wishes. Jennifer and Sandy settled in, ready for an all-nighter.

"We have one suspect with a timeline connection who could've known about that secret door," Jennifer announced.

She cleared the coffee table book off the table, giving me plenty of room to lay out and organize my Post-it notes. I had to love the way both she and Sandy anticipated my needs.

Sandy chewed on her thumbnail. "Players, stadium groundskeepers, office staff, and remodelers are potential suspects."

"Amanda said they looked for the door during the last remodel in 2002 but didn't find it," I replied.

"That limits our timeline to 1950–2002," Jennifer concluded.

Sandy whistled. "That's over fifty years." Talk about looking for that proverbial needle in a haystack.

"I'll pull the building permits and architectural drawings filed at City Hall in the morning. Someone built it. Determining when the door was installed and exactly where it went could lead us to the culprit."

79

"The stadium was smaller back then," I pointed out.

"It was also next to a lover's lane–style drive-in movie lot," Jennifer added.

"That was a thing?" I tried not to laugh at Sandy's grimace. Hard to believe that her generation had never experienced a rotary phone or a cassette either.

"I've never been to one, but Aunt Char tells stories about my dad and her in the back of a station wagon watching cartoons," I said.

Jennifer nodded. "The drive-in scene with John Travolta in *Grease* was classic." On her tablet she displayed a grainy black-and-white photo showing a row of the iconic flowing lines and futuristic tail fins of 1950s vehicles facing a big screen that was seemingly mounted to the Barkview Cliffs.

I shared a glance with Sandy. Since we'd found tunnels on the north side of town near the lagoon, locating more tunnels hidden in the sealed-off Barkview Cliffs' caves seemed very possible. My heart thumped just thinking about that crazy adventure during an earthquake. "Find out if any tunnels were discovered behind the screen."

Champ's sudden bark didn't slow my pulse. When he jumped to his feet and scurried to the garage door, I knew Russ was home. Champ was better than an alarm system. Tail slapping against the door frame, the dog blocked Russ's entrance with offensive line efficiency until my husband balanced a familiar glossy white fiberboard retail box atop his briefcase to scratch that wiggling butt.

He should've known better. I leaped in just as he sneezed, saving the tumbling box from a sure catastrophe. Nell's warm, gooey, peanut-butter-and-M&M monster cookies deserved white-glove attention.

"That was too close." Jennifer relieved me of the box.

Sandy hovered around the granite countertop while

80

Jennifer set out the cookies and napkins. Barely fitting on a dessert-sized plate, the cookies with their bumps of colorful M&M's had Sandy salivating with Pavlovian intensity. That she could eat whatever she wanted and stayed so slim and in shape really annoyed me.

"Yum-m-m-y," Sandy crooned like a kid in a candy store. "You know your way to a girl's heart, Russ."

"My pleasure. Couldn't let the team go hungry." On the surface, Russ's crooked smile looked good-guy genuine. He even offered Champ his own special treat. The dog inhaled it and thanked him by offering a paw to shake. Instead of returning to his spot in front of the fireplace, he remained where he was, a barrier between Russ and me.

The Lab sensed the same thing I did. There'd been more to Russ's stop at Nell's than picking up treats—something I doubted I'd like. A lingering whiff of that liver treat replaced the smell of sweet peanut butter cookies and turned my stomach. I wished we were alone.

Russ did too. I could tell from his frown as he washed his hands. He looked tired—exhausted, really—likely mirroring Uncle G.

"Have you figured out how the secret door works yet?" I asked quickly.

"No. We have a C-Thrue concrete scanner arriving in the morning." Russ dried his hands on a colorful flour sack towel. I handed him two of Barkview's special dog allergy pills. He smiled his thanks, leaned over the dog, and then turned my face toward his for a kiss. "We'll talk later," he whispered against my lips.

Talk about a prelude to bad news. I stiffened. I really wasn't going to like this conversation.

CHAPTER 9

Sandy and Jennifer shared a knowing glance and quickly finished their cookies. They left with dog excuses and promises to continue digging.

"That was awkward." I waved off the glass of shiraz-du-jour Russ offered me. I needed all my wits for this conversation.

"Only you thought so."

Might as well pull off the Band-Aid. "Why did you visit Nell?"

Russ sat on the bar-height chair and took a long swallow of wine. Champ's head rested on his knee. Who said dogs didn't show favoritism? I wasn't envious. Really. I walked him, picked up after him, took him to events, and fed him. Russ brought home a treat... Okay. Maybe I was a little envious.

"I questioned RJ Ruff this afternoon," Russ began. "He recruited me to coach the youth baseball team he sponsors. I think the boys are seven."

"Couldn't say no?" I smiled. Watching Russ run around a diamond in tight baseball pants worked for me.

"Talk to him. He's a charismatic salesman. See what your intuition tells you," Russ added.

"You think something's off?"

"I don't know. The thought of coaching impressionable kids and their overcompetitive parents might be clouding my judgment."

I didn't ask why. Russ's famous insight was rarely mistaken. "I don't doubt it. The man owns a Pug," I said.

That got his attention. "What does that mean, exactly?"

"The dog doesn't fit his persona. Pugs are excitable and stand out."

Russ failed to hide his laughter. "Not every owner looks like or behaves like their dog."

Danny Woofman and his Chihuahua came to mind. "Yeah, but you'd think a conservative guy who loves kids' sports would have a hound of some sort—you know, something kids could relate to."

"Isn't that a little stereotypical?"

Maybe. I still knew I was right. "Not a good enough reason to have someone watching him?"

Russ nodded. "Not for his dog choice. His refusal to name his anonymous buyer is another story."

"Is client confidentiality legal in this case?" He wasn't a doctor, lawyer, or priest.

"The chief threatened to charge him with criminal obstruction."

I bit back a smile. "The cuffs didn't break him."

"Nope. He did name a few local collectors and offered insight into the people interested in the Candy Catcher baseball card, though." Russ took my hand. "Nell was one of them."

No way. Not my all-night confidante. "She doesn't have that kind of money."

"According to RJ, Nell has tradables of equal value."

"She admitted she has a valuable Mickey Mantle card. I still can't believe childhood memories can be worth that much."

"The chief said the same thing. According to RJ, collecting tradables is a big business," Russ replied.

"You make it sound like an addiction," I said.

"A fair description, it turns out. Nell got very defensive when I spoke to her."

The same reaction I'd gotten when I'd discussed the baseball card with her. It made no sense, unless... "Is Mel involved?" Nell's younger sister always brought out my friend's momma-bear instincts. The fiery redhead had obsessive-compulsive covered. She'd proven that during the Howard Looc murder investigation.

Russ rhythmically stroked Champ's head. "That makes sense."

"Mel is impetuous, but I can't believe she'd hurt anyone, especially Ella." Mel's hotheadedness wouldn't extend to hurting a young girl.

"I agree. She doesn't have the temperament."

"She might have stolen the baseball card, though," I mused, "if she believed it didn't rightfully belong to the museum." How that could be possible I had no idea, but it was worth asking Nell about.

"I agree. I thought it was interesting that Champ led us to a potential hidden door today," said Russ.

"Me too. He's a retriever, not a scent hound."

"Which makes me curious exactly how Champ knew it was there."

He'd verbalized my thoughts exactly. "Yes. Unless Champ recognized the man." Russ saw patterns where others didn't. I didn't entirely understand how, but his results demanded respect. I closed my eyes, replaying the card-signing scenes in my mind. No one stood out. "He's met so many people in

84

Barkview. It could be anyone. I know how you feel about coincidences." Russ didn't believe in them. Experience had taught me not to question luck. Secrets tended to reveal themselves when they were ready. "Do you think who Ella saw is related to the missing Candy Catcher baseball card?"

"I don't know." Frustration laced his tone. "A passage through the museum that passes right by the Fab Five display where the bat found at the crime scene was displayed does suggest a connection."

My pulse jumped. "Champ's necklace at the crime scene indicates the person had been close to the dog too. But why go back after the card's been stolen?"

Russ sneezed, displacing Champ and releasing another puff of black hair. I cringed. The dog's needle-like hairs had embedded themselves everywhere.

"Who else was at the stadium when she saw the intruders?" I asked.

Russ blew his nose and checked his tablet. "The players and coaching staff were on the field. Two trainers were in the locker room."

"Was Officer Richards' cousin there too?" I asked.

"Not that I know of. As far as we can tell, no one was in the parking lot either."

That no-outdoor-surveillance-camera ordinance proved problematic today. "How long does it take to replace a window?"

"An hour? Maybe less. Why?"

"Danny Woofman was at the stadium replacing the foul ball window when I dropped Ella off."

Russ pulled his phone from his waist clip and typed. "I'll let the chief know. Maybe Woof saw something." A second later, his full attention refocused on me, his blue eyes searching. "What's your intuition telling you?"

I exhaled. He really did read me too well. "Someone connected to the Fab Five is involved. I'd say Clark Sugarland is my number one suspect."

No laughter, not even a conciliatory smile. "Keep pursuing the Fab Five angle. I'll dig deeper into the parties interested in purchasing the baseball card." Champ's yawn drew mine and Russ's. "Is Champ's dog bed in the trunk of your car?"

I nodded. "It's bulky..."

"I'll bring it in. We'll introduce him to his place on the floor at the foot of the bed and see how it goes."

"Like that ever stopped Renny from jumping in bed."

"We've had dogs in bed with us before," Russ added.

Sharing our bed with a full-sized, sneeze-inducing Labrador seemed a whole lot different than the two burrowing Dachshunds I'd dog-sat a few months ago. My husband's acceptance should've been good news, yet it bothered me. Was he really soft on discipline or just a pragmatist dealing with this temporary situation? The answer mattered.

Russ sneezed despite taking the allergy pills. Strike that. No matter what Champ did, this wasn't going to end well for me.

CHAPTER 10

Champ didn't give our bed a second look. Why would he? His orthopedic memory foam dog bed on the floor seemed more comfortable than our king-sized one. Any wonder he climbed in and went right to sleep. Who knew a dog needed tailored support to sleep? Not that the technology mattered. The bat dog snored worse than my seriously congested husband. I know; I heard them both snoring in tandem all night long. Almost all night. I must've dozed right before dawn because not only did I miss Russ getting up, but I slept through my blaring alarm until Champ's face-lick woke me with a start.

Never good when jolted awake, I felt like I was drowning in the generous dog slobber on my cheek. I catapulted out of bed, missing Champ's paw by a hair, not because of agility on my part, but Champ's sixth sense. He jerked it to safety. I then slipped on the leopard throw rug and skated across the wood floor in a slapstick Hollywood moment destined to go viral. Banging my head on the bathroom door didn't help my caffeine-starved headache any either, but it did motivate me. I had barely thirty minutes to meet Aunt Char at the bank, and Champ needed to go out. Why else would he be pacing at the door?

Champ paid the price for my tardiness. He let me know my two wimpy ball tosses weren't up to his usual standards with a noteworthy snort. To my surprise, a treat bribe didn't redeem me. Seriously? What dog didn't forgive anything for treats? Not this one. Although he jumped into my Jag's front seat, his unblinking scrutiny promised retribution.

"Get in line," I muttered as I straightened the French cuffs beneath my blue tweed blazer sleeves and walked around my car to the driver's side. I tested the speed limit down the Terraces' twisty-turny road into town and sped past the iconic Old Barkview Inn. I saw Canine Caramel's 1950s retail candy shop located on the corner as I turned right onto Sycamore and made a mental note to visit the factory after the bank. A block east loomed the stately Victorian bank in the wispy fog. Built in 1901, the pale-yellow shingled and gray-gabled building honored Barkview's rich past and promising future.

Maybe not so promising today. Trepidation trickled the length of my spine as I parked in front of Aunt Char's Mercedes. What secrets would be uncovered in the Sugarland family vault?

Champ sensed something too. He set the pace at a jog up the two stone steps to the glass door. I didn't need to knock. A single big-dog rumble announced my arrival. Although the bank was equipped with a Russ-approved security system, Brutus and Caesar, twin take-you-down, fawn-colored Bullmastiffs, protected the door like generations of their ancestors had before them. Weighing in at one hundred and thirty-plus pounds, those drooling muscle machines had paws that likely required horseshoes. Picking up their daily poop pile... My hand formed into a Champ-sized load. Ugh. The Lab weighed less than half of what the Mastiffs did. I'd need a lawn-and-leaf bag.

The trash bag vision helped. Although I'd come a long way from running for cover every time I saw a dog with big bicuspids, I still rubbed my neck scar, my forever reminder of the bite that changed my life.

The bank's manager, Jesse James (not exactly an inspiring vote of financial confidence), unlocked and opened the door.

"Welcome, Mrs. Cat. We are ready for you."

At least he hadn't chided me for tardiness. I felt Champ's unease as if he'd spoken directly to me. Not that I blamed him. The massive Mastiffs took some getting used to. Fortunately, Aunt Char had not included Renny, keeping the canine hierarchy in balance.

I stroked the bat dog's head. "Nothing to worry about." Champ's you-can't-be-serious look made me laugh. It worked for the Lab. He shook his head and matched my stride, sniffing every step we took.

"Good morning, my dear. I see you and Champ managed last night." My aunt kissed my cheek and scratched Champ's ears.

Although impeccably dressed in cream-colored Dior, she looked tired. Guilt stirred. She had enough on her plate. "I'm sorry to do this to you."

"It's best I know the truth. Let us get what we came here for and let Jesse get to it." Aunt Char marched toward the main vault. Without a word, Jesse trailed behind.

Champ and I dutifully followed my aunt through the massive, metal-framed vault doorway into an area filled with endless rows of dark metal boxes in various shapes and sizes. The Barkview Bank had built their newer vault around the original bank boxes. The last time I'd been in this same vault, my need-to-know meter had gone into overload. "What I wouldn't give to know what's in some of these boxes."

The same curiosity glittered in Jesse's gray eyes. Being surrounded by secrets daily would drive me crazy.

"Be careful what you ask for." Aunt Char's comment struck a chord.

I twisted my leopard-print neck scarf. Digging up secrets tended not to be particularly safe. "Think of all the Barkview time capsules in here."

My comment didn't even draw my aunt's attention. "I sometimes wonder if that which one generation deems valuable would hold the same importance to the current generation."

True. Was it monumental secrets or a bygone era's junk? The reporter in me still wanted to find out for myself.

Aunt Char handed Jesse a box key. The bank manager confirmed the number and led us to a midsize box. He inserted the bank's master key and then Aunt Char's into the lock and slid the metal box from the wall. "If it makes you feel any better, this box has been accessed often over the years," Jesse said.

I'd feel better after I read the documents. Aunt Char and I followed Jesse to the well-appointed viewing room. "Let me know when you are ready to return the box to the vault," he told us, and left.

I nodded. Little more than a cubicle, the postage-stamp-sized room did have a black leather executive chair and cherry wood desk equipped with a high-magnification reading glass for inspecting documents.

Aunt Char sat in the chair while I leaned over her shoulder, inhaling her Chanel perfume. I'd half-hoped to find the remaining baseball cards neatly tied together with a bow when she opened the box. No such luck. A single legal-sized envelope with Aunt Char's name in Grandma K's script filled the space.

Without even an iota of hesitation, Aunt Char tore open the envelope and removed two handwritten notes. She read the first out loud.

I never wanted my request to be a burden, dear Charlotte. But if you are reading this, Ella is in danger. As you have no doubt surmised, the Fab Five baseball cards were not destroyed. Only the lives they touched.

The Fab Five's secrets were buried in the fire. My brother swore he didn't start it, but someone did, and the ball players were all there. Karl bullied the boys to secrecy and rebuilt Canine Caramel with a single-mindedness born from guilt. Years later, redemption failed.

The answers are in the cards. Reunite them, my friend, and right their wrongs.

It is the only way for all involved to be freed.

Yours, Kandy

Aunt Char and I exhaled in unison. A Barkview hero knocked off his pedestal and a family's honor destroyed in one note. The Candy Catcher's reach for redemption meant the original players all knew about the baseball cards.

The answers were in the past.

Aunt Char unfolded and handed me the second note. It was a list, dated 1982.

~~Artie Wilcox~~
~~Bertie Wallace~~
~~Joe Sullivan~~
Mary Smith

Why wasn't Owen Daniels's name on the list, and who the heck was Mary Smith?

CHAPTER 11

Grandma K's revelations utmost in my mind, Champ sat in the passenger seat beside me as I headed east on Sycamore toward Canine Caramel's production plant in the Barkview Industrial Complex. Of course, I contacted Sandy and asked her to look into Mary Smith. Not that she'd be easy to find. Mary Smith had to be the most common name in America.

The emptiness of the Sugarlands' box struck me. A single letter and a list? Every hundred-year-old family had a skeleton or three. There had to be another hiding place. The candy factory seemed a likely possibility.

Built in the 1950s to accommodate the post–World War II population boom, the hillside acreage located on the east side of Interstate 5 had an abundance of stately Torrey pines that had dictated the twists and turns in the road. Nearly blinded by the morning sun, I dropped the driver's side visor as I zigzagged past several nothing-but-business concrete structural warehouses, finally arriving at the Victorian-fronted Canine Caramel factory. Constructed after the fire, the tan-shingled entry trimmed with white gingerbread occupied a prime double lot with a Bark Rock view.

Inside, I felt like I'd stepped into a time warp. The mid-century modern furnishings included Danish sofas and chairs. Photos of award-winning confections decorated the walls. The mouthwatering caramel apples looked so real I swear I smelled the comforting aroma of melted caramel. Of course, the silver bowl overflowing with individually wrapped samples drew me like a beacon as I approached the reception desk. I unwrapped and popped one into my mouth. I'd missed breakfast. "Yum. These are sinfully good. How do you not weigh three hundred pounds?"

The petite, white-haired woman's dimpled smile welcomed me. "After the first month, you never eat another one. After twenty years smelling sugar..." She wrinkled her nose. "Carrots are my go-to."

I'd be a diabetic. Me, get tired of sweet treats? Never.

Champ nudged my leg. No misunderstanding his tongue out pant. He couldn't possibly be hungry. He'd eaten before we'd left the house. Fortunately, the receptionist offered him one of her carrots. The dog gobbled it in a single motion.

"Is Clark available? Tell him I've brought Champ so he can practice the ball transfer with the dog for tomorrow's game." Not exactly my main goal, but it sounded better than "I dropped in to interrogate him."

The woman dialed his office. She covered the mouthpiece, but I heard her anyway. "No, sir. I don't see the appointment on your calendar either. Yes, the dog is here."

For a minute I doubted Clark would see me. Like many Barkview business leaders, Clark Sugarland and I attended many of the same charity events. Other than exchanging greetings, we'd never really talked. His rocky relationship with my aunt didn't help any either.

Time to stress eat. I reached for another caramel.

Loud enough for me to hear, she said, "Mr. Sugarland will see you." She pointed toward the elevator.

"I've toured the retail store but have never been here before."

The woman didn't seem surprised. Made me wonder how many visitors Clark had. "Straight ahead at the end of the hall. You can't miss it."

I thanked her with a smile and gave her a signed baseball card. My reporter instincts told me she had a story to tell.

Her blush said it worked. "Thank you. He's a beauty. Mr. Henry planned to include a bat dog in the Barkers' lineup before he died." She took a long breath.

"Really?" That was five years ago. "Why didn't the new GM execute the bat dog plan?" It made perfect sense in Barkview.

"I think there were some logistical issues and something about the players being upstaged."

Which could easily happen. The remark about logistics seemed odd.

The woman blinked away tears. "Many things changed after Mr. Henry was gone."

"You worked for Mr. Henry?" I asked the obvious question to keep her talking.

She nodded. "He was a good man. Hard, but fair, and he embraced change."

Unlike Clark. Call it manipulation, but I nudged Champ behind the woman's desk. The dog understood and dropped his head on her leg, somehow not disturbing the snow-white Havanese lounging in her lap. "So, what needs to be done?" I asked.

"Your aunt can't give up." Like the steady flow of a choco-late fountain, her words rolled off her tongue. "Everyone knows the manufacturing lines need to be upgraded. The old enrober can't keep up."

"The what?" I had to ask.

"It's the machine that chocolate-coats the caramel candy. It's down more than it operates. We're late on orders. Quality is"—she huffed—"not up to Sugarland standards."

I felt her frustration. "Why won't Clark upgrade?" When it was stated so clearly and passionately, how could he refuse?

The woman gestured toward the 1950s ode to the TV series *Happy Days* in the lobby. "The man lives in the past. His son will listen. I just hope there's something left for him and Miss Ella to take over."

For Ella's sake, I hoped so too. Discontent in the ranks never boded well. Was Clark so set in his ways that he didn't see it, or didn't he care?

The answer stared me down the moment the elevator doors opened on the second floor and the life-sized, formal portraits of Karl and his father, both tall and well-muscled with the same unsmiling determination. If not for the era-specific hair styles and clothing, I'd think they were twins.

A shrine to egomaniacs or over-the-top family pride? Why Clark's portrait hadn't joined his predecessors on the wall intrigued me. Instead, colorful product photos documenting the company's evolution lined the long hall leading to his office. Like the receptionist said, there was no missing it. I felt like a mail-order bride walking down the aisle.

Clark Sugarland's unwelcoming frown didn't make the trek any easier. Unlike his athletic ancestors, he was thin to the point of appearing gaunt. The stark white lab coat and hair net covering thinning gray hair washed out his already pale complexion and made his Schnauzer brows even more pronounced. "Is Ella all right?"

His obvious concern raised his likability rating considerably.

"She's fine. Shook up, but resilient," I replied.

"She's a good kid. A lot like her father." Clark's easy answer seemed honest enough. "The chief tells me he doesn't know if it was a kidnapping attempt or not. I'm sure Ella's unhappy, but I'm the one who insisted she stay at home and under guard until we know for sure. I owe it to my brother to watch out for his only daughter."

I believed him. Despite Clark's financial needs, he still dropped a notch on my suspect list. "Henry passed awfully young," I remarked.

Clark nodded sadly. "Diabetes is a dangerous disease. The Sugarland family is plagued with it. The result of generations of sugarholics, I imagine."

The conversation died there in a socially awkward pause. I expected him to demand, "What can I do for you?" Stony silence caught me off guard.

I fell back on my plan. "You and Champ will be on the field together when you throw out the first pitch tomorrow. You need to do a run-through. Wouldn't want the dog to upstage you."

"In this town?" Another twitch of those bushy brows.

A chuckle slipped past my lips. Was that humor under all that gruff? "I'll give you that one. Nonetheless, we should try not to disappoint them."

His expression said *Good luck*, but he did step aside for me to enter his office. Its utilitarian style surprised me. While the lobby and hallway looked like his father had never left, this space felt fresher. Not modern, exactly. The dark wood bookshelves lining two walls and the matching executive wood desk with computer station did have a 1990s look. The addition of dual computer screens, a tablet, a radio, and a phone helped modernize the look. I envied the lack of paper piles on his desk. The order made the two framed photos, one of his son's young family and the other of a Schnauzer, stand out. No candy jar made sense, but I'd still been looking forward to another taste. To the right of the desk, French doors with Levolor blinds opened onto a balcony overlooking the candy factory.

Curiosity drew me to the door. "I love your caramels. Mind if I take a look?" I gave him little choice.

My hand was already on the doorknob when he said, "Please keep Champ inside. For health reasons, he can't be in the production area."

Good point. Flying fur sticking to chocolate caramel apples did more than turn my stomach. Champ got it too; he sat beside a desk chair.

I opened the door to Loompaland. Of course, the factory wasn't painted like a cartoonish garden, nor were small people employed there, but the sweet scent of caramelizing sugar and dark chocolate made all my childhood memories wrap around me like a familiar hug. Up here, I felt like the queen of the sugar mountain.

Visually, the warehouse looked more like a hospital operating room than a Hollywood candy plant. White lab coats stood beside pink ones while a hairnet rainbow added more color. The white beard guards covered more than half the men's faces and looked decidedly uncomfortable. A good reason to shave off facial hair, for sure. Despite its obvious age, the machinery did sparkle like new. The pride in ownership showed in the stainless-steel's mirror-like shine and color-fully-painted parts.

"Wow! Some of that stuff looks ancient," I said, leaning against the railing. "Did your grandfather install it all after the fire?"

"Some of it. The caramel apple vats weren't added until 1963. Dan Walker, who worked for Kraft Foods, introduced the concept..."

The hunch in Clark's back disappeared along with his monotone. He really did have passion bottled up under all that structure. "I bet this was your father's favorite place."

He nodded. "Dad liked to survey his kingdom. I remember standing here. I was twelve when he said, 'Some day you will be responsible for all of this. Make me proud.'"

In that moment I understood. "Your life changed that day. I'll never forget when Aunt Char told me my destiny."

My honesty must've struck a chord. Clark smiled—a lip lift, really. "What did you want to be before?"

His question spoke volumes. "A Pulitzer Prize–winning reporter on the international desk," I replied without hesitation. My dreams had changed, though. I loved Barkview. "Where's your happy place?"

"The La Brea Tar Pits," he admitted.

Dinosaurs versus candy making. Talk about different worlds. No wonder he masked shyness behind curtness.

"Everyone says how lucky we are, but you understand," Clark said.

I did. All too well. "We are lucky. We have responsibilities they"—I put "they" in air quotes—"will never understand, but we have choices." I stopped his rebuttal with my forefinger. "We can make the job what we want it to be."

He considered my answer. "Is that why Jennifer is your GM?"

I nodded. "I'm not great at day-to-day operation. I'm a freelance reporter at heart. My advice is to be honest with yourself about your talents and dreams. Don't let this"—I gestured toward the factory—"stop you."

His smile seemed genuine and brightened his dull expression. "Easier said than done."

"I'm a work in progress." I turned serious again. "We're alike, you know, both following strong, decisive leaders. I will never be my aunt, but I will leave my mark."

He considered my words for a moment. "I have no doubt you will. I appreciate your candor. Now, why are you really here?"

Clark was a lot of things. A fool was not one of them. I went with honesty. "Tell me about the fire. I understand it started in the caramel cookers."

My question surprised him. "That's the theory. No one knows for sure. I'm just glad no one was hurt," Clark said.

"How is it possible that a vat of caramel could catch fire? Wouldn't the afternoon shift have cleaned it?"

"They should have. It was seventy years ago. Our safety and hygiene protocols are better now." Clark frowned. "Why do you care? It was a long time ago."

"The company was in financial trouble back then. It needed updating."

"Similar to now. Yes," Clark replied without hesitation.

"The insurance money was fortuitous."

"I'm not sure my father agreed. The Candy Catcher made it to the major leagues."

"He lived his dream," I said.

"He tasted it for three years. In a way, I think that's worse. I admire what my dad sacrificed for this company," Clark admitted.

And drilled into his son. "He owned a baseball team. See what I mean about making it work? He continued to be involved in baseball as a coach and owner."

Clark nodded. Enlightened? Maybe.

"What did your dad say about the fire?" I asked.

"Not much. Nana Dolce always said that dad's destiny was decided when the fire destroyed the baseball cards."

My intuition alerted. "But the Candy Catcher's card wasn't destroyed. When did you find it?"

"Grandma K found it in my father's papers after his death in 1992. I found out about it when she passed."

"Why did Grandma K keep the card secret for over twenty years?" I had to ask.

"I don't know. I would've thought she'd have donated it to the museum years ago."

I agreed. Something had changed. Finding out what it was mattered, so I dropped my mini-bomb. "It's been suggested that the Candy Catcher card was not the only card to survive the fire."

Clark exhaled. "That rumor has been going around since I was a kid."

"There have been reports of secret auctions," I added.

"Yet, no one has admitted to seeing those supposed other cards." He sounded too sure of himself. Did he know more? "I take it you've been looking for them too."

I shrugged. "Why do you want to close down the baseball card museum?"

"I see Amanda has been talking too much." Clark massaged the bridge of his nose. Perhaps he was choosing his words carefully. "I haven't made any decisions on the subject. That is a business decision between Amanda and me. And yes, if authenticated Fab Five cards did come up in auction, I would bid on them. Not because I value the cards, but because of what they mean to Barkview."

I believed him. Whatever his gripe about the museum, the Fab Five baseball cards weren't the issue. I did wonder where he'd get the money, though.

CHAPTER 12

Much as I wanted to pursue the hunt for the baseball card, Champ's celebrity status came first. What can be more important than paw-o-graphing baseball cards at a posh convention anyway?

There was no point in fighting my celebrity PR role. It wasn't Champ's fault that a crisis had struck Barkview. I did avert my gaze from the KDOG office as I drove by. The paper mountains covering the wood grain of my desk did not affect daily operations, but I would pay the price later.

I turned left on First Street. On my right, with the Pacific Ocean as the backdrop, the elegant sky-blue, white-gingerbread-trimmed Old Barkview Inn peeked through the coastal fog. Hands down the most photographed building in Barkview, the late-Victorian-era structure had hosted countless Hollywood productions featuring the iconic beachfront widow's walk connecting twin turrets.

I drove under the lattice-trimmed portico and stopped in the valet lane. The moment I removed Champ's jersey from his bag, the Lab sat taller on the passenger seat. He knew it was time to work, I realized, and he made it easier for me. Instead of jumping out of my vehicle the moment the valet opened the door, intent on mischievous exploration like the other dogs I'd cared for, the bat dog waited patiently for me to slip the jersey over his head. He offered his right paw and then the left to expedite the process. Champ even head-nudged me, reminding me to add the baseball cap. Talk about a real-life Superman costume.

This was one amazing dog. For the first time, I walked up the hotel's grand marble steps and entered the Old Barkview Inn accompanied by a dog with no concern that the hand-carved mahogany molding and ocean-inspired stained-glass windows would suffer consequences.

Champ did pause in the lobby, his nose sniffing intently skyward. I took a moment to join him. The smell of beeswax and aged fine wood would forever remind me of this grand lady of a hotel. Today, I bypassed the concierge desk, glad that Franklin, the concierge extraordinaire, was half-hidden behind a glossy foldout map directing a guest. Not that Franklin wasn't helpful—the man did take service to a level five-star resorts coveted—but when seeking information relating to the inn, my best source had to be Will Oldeman, the longest continuous employee and the most well-informed.

Champ followed my lead as I headed across the polished wood foyer to the Centurion Otis 61 elevator. Originally powered by steam, the ornate wrought iron museum piece had been converted to electric in the early 1970s.

Dressed in starched dark tails and a striped waistcoat, the ancient elevator operator stood at his post with a pride that went deeper than longtime employment.

"Welcome, Mrs. Cat. It is a pleasure to meet you, Master Champ." The Lab leaned directly into Will's ear scratch.

Champ's doggy smile drew mine. He liked Will. "You were

103

only a kid back then, but do you know anything about a secret door at Barker Field?"

Will's Groucho brows arched. "You know about Grand Slam Alley?"

I squelched the vision of scantily clad women. "This goes back to the 1950s, the era of poodle skirts and saddle shoes."

"Morality was different back then, but boys will be boys." Had to love an impish grin on a seventy-year-old.

"How do you know about this?" The man really did know everything about Barkview.

"My uncle was a bat boy back in 1950–1952." Will stroked Champ's head, his dog loyalty tested. "Couldn't hold a candle to you, boy."

Will's pooch loyalty overrode family this time. "Where did this door lead to?"

"A bedroom built into an old storage area in the locker room."

A cheesy man's bedroom came to mind. "Who had access to it?"

"The week's top home run hitter."

I got the not-so-veiled reference as well as exactly where the dating references to first base, second base, and third base came from. "Do you know how to open it?"

Will shook his head. "My uncle and another bat boy searched for it years later. They never found the hidden door. Only those in the select fraternity had the privilege."

An elite group at best. "Like the Fab Five?" No wonder those guys hit so well. I waited for Will's nod before adding, "I suspect Karl Sugarland, uh, used it."

"Yeah. Often. The Candy Catcher batted .556 senior year. My uncle called him a hound dog."

Another disparaging remark about this Barkview icon. How many other people had less-than-complimentary stories to tell about the man? "How is it that he's remembered as an upstanding Barkview citizen?"

"Adult redemption," Will explained. "I remember my mother saying that he changed his ways after the caramel factory fire. She was friends with Owen's mother, the first baseman badly hurt in a car accident the same night as the fire. There was talk about a jinx on the five. Sully, the shortstop, was hurt in an accident during his first year in the majors. He went on to become a Vegas showman."

"Really?"

"Yeah. His father never accepted it. He trained Sully to be a woodworker."

"Sully's father was a builder?" My intuition pinged.

"A good one too." Will gestured toward the carved banisters going up the stairs. "He did a lot of repair work at the Inn. Young Sully apprenticed with him until he made it in baseball."

The man had to have been an artisan to do the intricate work here. It begged the question, could Sully have built the secret entry? I scribbled a Post-it. Learning more about his father's construction projects seemed imperative.

"Sully's mother wanted him to do renovation work in Barkview. He stayed in Vegas. Only returned for his mother's funeral."

"Why?" The more I learned about the Fab Five, the more questions I had. Mostly surrounding Karl Sugarland. Did any of the men deserve Barkview's high praise?

"No one ever said. I remember my uncle saying Owen used the room frequently, too."

"I thought he was a nice guy." Was there a standup guy in the group?

"He was...before the accident. Owen had a serious girlfriend. I think she was a naval officer's daughter. Beautiful girl. He gave her his class ring." Will scratched his head.

I pictured a heavy man's ring on a chain. "Her father didn't approve?" It wasn't really a question. Back then, playing baseball wasn't considered a career. I wonder how Russ would feel about it even today if his daughter married a professional athlete. If he ever had one. Someday. I hoped.

"I suspect not. After the accident, she visited him in the hospital. They say she dumped him as soon as she realized his career was over." Will's sour-pickles lips took disapproving looks to a new level. "Broke a mirror when she threw Owen's class ring at him. Seven years bad luck and good riddance, I say."

Loyal Will. There was more to that story. I sensed it. "Do you know her name?"

"No. Don't want to either," Will huffed. "Does the door have something to do with what happened to Ella?"

I chewed my lip. Uncle G had frozen information. "What happened to Ella?"

"Keke said someone tried to kidnap her."

I crossed my arms. Ella's drama queen mother in action. "For Ella's sake, I hope you kill this info."

Will nodded. "The kid deserves some peace."

"Any guests at the baseball card convention of interest?" Subtlety had no place with Will. We both appreciated directness.

Will motioned me to come closer. I obeyed. This had to be some secret. "Mr. Ruff is in the Windsor Suite."

My pulse jumped. "Seriously?" I didn't doubt Will. It just made no sense. "Why? RJ lives less than two miles from here." I should know. I drove by his house every day on my way to and from town.

Will sniffed. "Mr. Ruff has been holding court."

The visual stuck. Much as I was afraid to ask, I had to. I found a Post-it pad and, hallelujah, a pen. Will seemed stunned. He hesitated a moment before repocketing his. "Who has seen him?"

I scribbled each name Will gave me. Truthfully, no name stood out until...

"Miss Mel? Nell's sister?" I knew it. My friend's defensiveness made perfect sense now. "Was Mel alone?"

"Yeah. Snuck up the back stairs when she thought I wasn't looking." Will gave me the two-fingers my-eye-is-on-you gesture. "Never miss a thing."

No doubt. "Why?"

"She and Miss Nell are collectors."

As if that explained everything. Was I the only one who didn't get collecting? Sure, I liked jewelry. I bought every unique sea-themed piece I found. But the thought of sneaking around to acquire more? I clearly needed to speak with Nell. There had to be more to this. "Anyone else?"

His voice dropped to a whisper. "Officer Richards' cousin is supposedly a sports memorabilia dealer too."

"Hunter Richards is a direct competitor of RJ Ruff's?" Not exactly incriminating. I collaborated with my colleagues at competing periodicals often. The way Will said it caught my attention though. Could Hunter be representing the anonymous bidder for the Candy Catcher card RJ Ruff had been protecting?

"Maybe. I tell you, Hunter Richards is up to something," Will insisted.

"Why?" I had to ask.

"He's friendly—too friendly, if you ask me."

"I bet he's popular with the ladies." Any man that ruggedly handsome would be.

Will acknowledged that truth with a reluctant nod. "He asks a lot of questions."

So did I. Did that make me suspicious too? "What kind of questions?"

"Personal kinds. He also sits in the lobby reading the paper every morning. Says he likes the feel of it."

"I do too." No crime in that. As a publisher I appreciated the sentiment. The Old Barkview Inn still took daily delivery of the *Wall Street Journal* and *Los Angeles Times*, in addition to the *Bark View*. "What's suspicious about that?"

"His reading glasses are reflective."

I made a note of Will's knowing whisper. "Who's he watching?"

"The triathlete from Dallas staying in the Queen's Crossing Suite. His name's Austin Bruns. The man runs on the ocean boardwalk every morning and then drinks a smoothie in the lobby around 8:30 a.m."

"What do you know about the triathlete?" I asked.

"Family owns breweries and sports bars."

"He's here to buy memorabilia for his restaurants?" That kind of made sense. I needed to chat with him. "How will I recognize him?"

"You will."

Will's certainty resonated. This guy must be a character if I could pick him out without a picture-perfect description. I didn't ask how Will had gathered his intel either. Truth be told, it didn't matter. "I'll listen for the accent."

"No need."

Turned out Austin Bruns, the tall Texan, sought me out the moment Champ and I entered the Old Barkview Inn's Crown Ballroom. Host to the baseball card convention, the regal octagonal room featured dark-paneled walls with marble-columned alcoves that had served as Hollywood throne rooms in too many movies to list.

Today, glass display cases twinkled beneath conical chandeliers filled with Cooperstown memorabilia. On a raised dais to the right, a comfortable wing-back chair and table invited celebrities to meet and greet their fans.

Champ knew the drill too well. After scouting the room, he doggedly dragged me to the dais. With close to a hundred folks in attendance, that proved problematic. Not for the three-foot-tall dog who wove through and around legs, but for me, who was greeted by practically everyone.

Champ tolerated the small talk with his usual patience until a tall, well-muscled man in a black cowboy hat blocked my path. "Ma'am." I craned my neck to meet his bold hazel eyes as the blond tipped his Stetson and extended his hand.

I blushed. Couldn't help myself. Southern charm got me every time. Normally, I found a five o'clock shadow to be unkempt. On Austin, it just looked rugged.

Before I could shake his outstretched hand, Champ nudged me aside. The dog's huff couldn't be called a growl, but the way his body created a no-nonsense barrier between us alerted me. Instinct told me to go with it. Something wasn't right about Mr. Bruns. Did the Lab sense a threat?

"If you'll excuse me. We have baseball cards to sign." With a quick wave, I scooted away.

The man's hand dropped to his side. Anyone left standing alone on the dance floor should be confused, maybe even annoyed. His arched brow stirred my unease. Needless to say, my gaze followed the bad-guy black cowboy hat around the room the entire time I stood beside Champ while he signed baseball cards. Prejudging rarely panned out, but I couldn't deny Hollywood's influence. Mr. Bruns was involved in this case. I could feel it.

CHAPTER 13

Sandy must've communicated my concerns to Russ because they both arrived thirty minutes after I texted her to look into Austin Bruns. Although the paw-o-graphing line started at the door, Russ and Sandy cut to the front.

Dressed in another Barkers baseball jersey and jeggings that showed off her enviable runner's legs, my assistant blended in with the convention crowd. She slipped between me and Champ and motioned toward Russ, who scratched the dog's ears. Wearing a black-striped polo shirt with a white collar, he looked decidedly umpire-ish.

"I got this. Do what you need to do," Sandy whispered.

Russ made the transition smooth. He kissed me with showy, knee-weakening expertise. "Where is Austin?" he whispered against my mouth.

It took me a minute to recover before I inclined my head toward a nearby alcove. "The guy with the cowboy hat." No need to say more. Austin stood out like a lone wolf in a pack of sheep.

Russ's phone pinged. He read, "Austin Bruns does acquire

sports-related merchandise for his family's bars. He has attended the last three memorabilia conventions."

"He could be RJ's anonymous bidder for the Candy Catcher card." Not that that in itself was incriminating.

"What did Champ do when he met Austin?" Russ asked.

"He acted like an overprotective husband." My chide was only half-teasing. I appreciated Russ's concern, but really, I could take care of myself.

"I'll have a chat with him." The promise in Russ's lip raise looked more like a bar fight brewing than a casual conversation.

Exactly what I didn't want him to do. Before I could temper his protective instincts, Austin materialized at our side. "Mr. and Mrs. Hawl, I have information you will find worth listening to."

Talk about an attention-getting line. Russ's situation assessment must've found nothing imminently threatening because he gestured for Austin to follow us toward the ocean-side bar. Any attempt at casual failed when Russ stepped between us and anchored his left arm on my shoulder, leaving his dominant hand free. I followed my husband's lead. What else could I do without causing a scene?

Austin selected a private table tucked into a corner with a panoramic view of Bark Rock. That I'd nearly been buried alive out there did cross my mind.

Russ duplicated Austin's craft beer order. I chose an iced tea with extra lemon. Drinking before noon required a midday nap, which wasn't going to happen with a little more than twenty-four hours remaining to find the stolen Candy Catcher card.

Austin waited for the drinks to be delivered before starting. "We are on a mutual quest."

A "quest" sounded so Arthurian. "You were one of the

anonymous bidders for the Candy Catcher card," I stated, relieved to demystify one secret when he inclined his head. "Why do you even want a Barkview baseball card?"

"The Fab Five's second baseman, Bertie Wallace, was my great-uncle. I know the original autographed five-card set exists."

I gasped. Didn't expect that one. Only one way he could know. "You have Bertie's card?" So, Grandma K's note had been true. All the cards had been saved.

"Did. My family started the brewery back in 2001 after Bertie passed," he explained. "My uncle found the card in Bertie's papers in an envelope marked "Payment." No idea why. The dot com crash nearly bankrupted the business. My uncle sold the card along with other collectibles to raise cash. That baseball card saved the company. Now, I'd like to acquire the set and display it at our flagship brewery."

A noble cause. "Do you know who bought Bertie's baseball card?"

"No. The buyer purchased through a broker and paid for anonymity. I hoped you might know."

The MO sounded familiar.

"Who brokered the deal?" Russ asked.

"RJ Ruff. Do you know who has the Owen card?"

I crushed his hopeful smile. "No." We didn't even know where the Candy Catcher card was. "Have you approached Sully's family for his baseball card?"

"Sully's granddaughter sold his card to another anonymous buyer to pay for her medical school tuition. She's a neurosurgeon now. Artie Wilcox's baseball card was donated in a box with other cards to a church bazaar back in 2010. No one knows who bought it, but I've offered a generous price to purchase it from the owner."

Two of the Fab Five's baseball cards had been sold for the

next generation's benefit to unknown buyers. No way that was a coincidence. Who else would buy up the Fab Five cards? "What do you want from me? I don't own the Candy Catcher card."

Austin stroked his jaw. "I hear Canine Caramel is in, uh, financial trouble."

Barkview's gossip machine needed taming. "I wouldn't know."

Austin didn't buy it. "I am prepared to be quite generous. In addition, the baseball card museum can keep the card on loan until our exhibits are finalized. Then I will agree to loan the museum the set for a specified time period." He winked at Russ. "It will require adequate security."

Russ's smile didn't reach his eyes.

"How long will it be before your exhibits are completed?" I admired the man's audacity.

"A year. Maybe longer."

I felt Russ stiffen. Was Austin just being a good Samaritan, or was he somehow involved? Ella had refused to sell the card before. How far would he go to get the Candy Catcher card? More importantly, did I believe his story?

Something about his answers seemed too convenient. Russ thought so too. He didn't fight Austin for the check.

The Texan paid the tab. "Please call me if I can be of assistance." Austin tipped his Stetson and left us standing at the bay window.

I ran my fingers through my bangs. "What next?"

"Keep looking." Russ didn't tell me to stay away from Austin. Which was telling.

"Two anonymous buyers after the same baseball card line intrigues me. I'll focus on the money trail."

The easy answer in every TV police procedural. I wondered

if it would pan out here. I glanced at my watch. Time to rescue Champ and Sandy from adoring fans.

I didn't need to look far. They both stood outside the bar entrance.

"Geez. That's hard work." Sandy had already removed Champ's jersey and scratched his back. "He was a champ."

No doubt. The Lab rubbed his head against my leg. I scratched his head. "Good boy." I felt missed.

"Champ deserves some fun," Sandy insisted.

I started to object. Locating the missing baseball card needed our focus, but Sandy jerked a six-inch mini-bat from the backpack slung over her shoulder. Of course, Champ saw it. A shot of energy rippled through his body, making his tail slap rhythmically against my leg. Caught up in his puppy-like enthusiasm, I laughed. No way I could deny him.

The little anticipatory hop in his step continued as we walked through the hotel and exited onto the boardwalk.

Sandy's javelin-thrower windup sent the bat on an end-over-end flight across the sand. Like a sprinter out of the blocks, the dog took off after it. He returned moments later to drop the bat at Sandy's feet and bark for more. Sandy threw it again. When he returned the second time, Champ dropped the bat at my feet.

The dog loved this. I picked up the mini-bat and threw it. Not as far as Sandy, but the shape seemed to help it along. "The bat's different."

"Michael invented the design for Champ. The knob and handle are about the same size as a standard bat, so it feels the same in Champ's mouth. The barrel is shorter, so it's easier to carry around," Sandy explained. "Champ loves it."

He sure did. The dog's energy burst made me tired. "How do you know dogs so well?"

"Dogs are not complicated. Champ is a retriever by nature.

He lives to retrieve anything. Over and over again. Unlike men."

Oh no. This wasn't about Champ. I understood her frustration too well. It's true, some of us had to kiss a lot of frogs before we found "the one." I had until Russ came along. I still couldn't understand how someone as gorgeous, intelligent, and kind as Sandy fell into the same category. Her last boyfriend had almost killed Aunt Char. "What happened?"

Sandy shook her head. "Jennifer and Gabby..."

No need to say more. "Set you up with Officer Richards' cousin, Hunter."

Her frown agreed. "More like orchestrated a meeting. Jennifer asked me to pick up a coffee for her when Hunter was at the Daily Wag."

Meeting anyone under Gabby's scrutiny could be daunting. "And? I saw him at the Sit and Stay Café. He's cute."

Sandy's shrug wasn't promising. "He seemed nice enough at first. He played college baseball. Has a sports medicine and kinesiology degree from Columbia. He even had a Jack Russell growing up."

He sounded perfect. Why didn't she sound more excited? "But?"

"I felt like he was reading a script. And suddenly he thanked me for my time and left." She exhaled.

My intuition twinged. "Maybe he had a meeting or something,"

"I'd have understood that, but he crossed Oak Street and got into a sedan about halfway down Fourth Street. He sat there watching the Daily Wag for thirty minutes."

Her confusion made sense. "Maybe he was on the phone."

"If he was, he didn't say anything. He was gone when I checked an hour later."

No one would have noticed him camping out a block away

from the coffee shop except Sandy. Her keen observation skills had helped me too many times. "Was Austin Bruns in the Daily Wag?"

"Yeah. He walked in right before Hunter left."

It all made sense now. Why did I ever question Will? The man was always right. "I'd stay away from Hunter for now," I suggested.

"No kidding. I don't need that kind of drama." She exhaled. "It's too bad. He was cute."

She had been interested. "Did you find out anything else?" Better to refocus her.

"There are like thirty thousand Mary Smiths in the US. I need more information to narrow the search. I also struck out on finding Owen's judgmental girlfriend. She gives all women a bad name. I can't imagine her dumping him because of his injury. Not someone you're prepared to marry."

"Could she be Mary Smith?" I asked.

"I don't know. I can tell you that no one named Mary Smith graduated from Bark U in the 1950s. There's no way to search the Bark U database for students with naval officers for fathers. There's no yearbook at the university either."

"And no social media posts." Even I lamented technology sometimes.

"It was a more peaceful time," Sandy admitted. "I also tried naval records for officers with the last name *Smith*. You have no idea how many there are. I forwarded my information to Russ. Maybe he or the chief will have better luck." She jerked her fingers through her hair. "I want to find her to chastise her. She ruined his life. Owen loved her."

I felt her frustration. "Someone must know something."

"Not one of the original Fab Five is still alive. I know they'd be ninety-something, but all five of them died before they were seventy," Sandy said.

"Someone must know something," I repeated.

"I tried Fab Five family members who might have known or heard of her. The most I've gotten is that hussy who broke poor Owen's heart. No one can remember her name."

Will had said essentially the same thing. I massaged the bridge of my nose. This was important. I sensed it. There had to be someone who remembered her, someone on the outside. "Keep looking. There's no other way to track down Owen's card." I filled her in on Austin's information.

"Owen died before Karl started giving away the cards," Sandy said. "He never married. He had no heirs. I can't find a Mary Smith in his past either. Who would Karl have given Owen's card to?"

I'd wondered that myself. Certainly not an ex-girlfriend who'd broken his friend's heart. Unless... We had to find that woman.

I'd planned to speak with RJ, but something told me that Nell knew something. Champ and I walked the five blocks to the Sit and Stay Café. The dog liked the exercise, and I needed to think. I'd been thinking the baseball card theft was motivated by greed. What if it was more than that? The crime scene had indicated the robbery had been personal. Why else use the Candy Catcher's bat? And what was Champ's tie-in?

Nell must've seen me coming because she waited for me at the door, watching me dodge the vehicles circling the popular lunch spot's parking area. She'd tied back her hair in a low ponytail that swished against the back of a vintage Barker jersey she wore beneath an apron featuring a painting of a black Labrador retriever. I recognized the tight lines around her mouth right away. She had something to tell me—something I wasn't going to like. Champ felt it too. He pressed against my side.

Despite the time, our number one Oak Street lunch spot

owner still motioned me to follow her around back. Set behind the Sit and Stay Café in a green-gabled carriage house, the Best Ingredients Snacks Barkery—BIS for short—invited customers through an award-winning stained-glass door showing dogs in epic flyball relays.

Champ's attention focused on the glass dogs. So much so that the heavy door tapped his butt, hurrying him inside as it shut behind us. More country kitchen than Victorian in décor, the barkery's charming gingham curtains and coordinating tablecloths, along with an old-fashioned picnic hamper display, always brought beach barbecues and family campouts to mind. Although Nell denied it, I swear they plumbed the aroma of Nell's killer cookies in here from the Sit and Stay Café.

Rolling pin in hand, dressed in a neat black chef's jacket with her flowing auburn hair pulled back in a ponytail, Mel looked like an industrious entrepreneur. Brisbane, her red Aussie, paced at her side. "W-what can I do for you?" Mel's emerald eyes darted from me to the door and back, while Brisbane paced. Fear or ADHD?

Hands on her hips, Nell looked like a disapproving momma. "Tell her what you know."

"I...uh..." A four-alarm fire burned on Mel's cheeks. "You told me to let it go."

"Let what go?" I asked.

Nell's frown scared me as much as it did her sister, who finally admitted, "Finding justice." Mel's pressed lips dared me to argue.

I didn't. Too many questions remained unanswered. I needed to deescalate the tension. "I think you'd better explain," I said.

My calmness worked. Mel exhaled before answering. "My aunt was the nurse who cared for Owen, the Fab Five's first baseman, for ten years before he died in 1982. She said his brain was stuck in 1952. He only talked about his glory days, which ended that year. He never married. So he left his baseball card collection to her. Owen's only request was that she deliver Karl a letter he'd written after his death."

Nell spoke. "Our Aunt Melanie, Mel's namesake, was a sweet lady." I got the inference.

So did Mel. She gnawed her lip. I expected a heated retort, not composure. "The memorabilia weren't worth much back then, but the stuff had sentimental value to our aunt since Owen had told her stories about the pieces."

"Which she documented," Nell added.

"You have her notes?" I asked. This sounded like another previously undiscovered Barkview treasure.

"Yes. Our aunt shared the stuff with another family member while they fought cancer. The collection is part of our family's history now," Mel explained.

No sense arguing that point. I cut to the chase. "Who do you think has the Owen baseball card?"

Silence hung between us. Finally Nell said, "Tell her what you think."

"I think Owen had an heir," Mel announced. "I think his girlfriend was pregnant when she left him at the hospital. Why else would she suddenly quit school, leave Barkview, and get married a few weeks later?"

My heart raced. It made too much sense. "You found her?" I asked.

"No. I tried, but only knowing her first name and that her dad was a Navy captain didn't lead anywhere."

"Was her name Mary?" I asked.

Mel's jaw dropped. "How did you know that?"

Nell saved me from answering. "You suspected the same thing."

No reason not to admit that. "It's possible. Morality was

different in 1952. Good girls didn't have children out of wedlock," I replied. "Owen could've even dumped her in his own despair and anger at the hospital."

Silence confirmed my statement. Mel spoke first. "We have to find her."

"She'd be in her nineties by now if she's still alive. Let's see what Sandy and Jennifer can find." Mel's obvious relief troubled me. I faced her squarely. Despite the risk, I had to know. "Did you steal the Candy Catcher card?"

"Steal! How could you think I... You mean it's missing?" Indignation aside, her undisguised pleasure bothered me. She knew something.

Her Aussie knew it too. He barked at her. The storm clouds in Nell's eyes made me step back. "Melanie Monique, enough. Ella's been threatened. If something happens to that young girl because of this baseball card, it's on you."

"I don't know anything about Ella. I swear it." Mel crossed her heart.

I believed her. "But you suspect who has the card."

Mel's clenched jaw confirmed my hypothesis. "I saw Officer Richards' cousin, Hunter, parked in that clump of sagebrush outside the stadium two nights ago around midnight. I always slow down there because Officer Richards likes to park with the speeding radar in the exact spot."

The timing fit. My intuition agreed. A supposed memorabilia dealer involved in clandestine meetings? Hunter Richards was up to something.

Nell massaged her forehead. "And what were you doing there, Mel?"

Good point. Mel's silence screamed guilt. She had been after the baseball card too.

"You know what? I don't want to know." Nell turned to me. "Arrest her for trespassing or attempted burglary or stupidity. I don't care what. Just get her out of my sight before I commit murder!"

Mel didn't wait around for my response. She shot out the door with her Aussie at her heels. Her parting words, shouted over her shoulder just before the glass door shook as it slammed, confused more than helped. "Hunter didn't know Xograph produced a 3-D card series for Kellogg's Corn Flakes."

"What is Xograph?" I asked.

Nell's spitting-nails anger wasn't directed at me, but I still stepped back. I'd never seen her quite this annoyed. "Xograph manufactured baseball cards back in the day. Ask RJ. I'm guessing my sister's telling you in her roundabout Mel way that Hunter Richards isn't who he says he is."

I'd guessed as much. "For Officer Richards' sake, I hope she's wrong." A police officer with a criminal cousin wouldn't help his career advancement any.

"She never is," Nell grumbled. She turned the sign on the barkery's door to read "Out to Lunch" and locked up. Champ and I followed her back to the café. "Your usual salad for lunch?"

My stomach growled my agreement. I'd had my suspicions about Hunter. Now I had something to go on.

CHAPTER 14

I knew better than to doubt Mel's eidetic memory, but acting without confirmation seemed silly. Sandy would want to know anything I discovered about Hunter Richards anyway.

She returned my call quickly. "Hunter Richards is a fraud." Her words spilled like water over Niagara Falls. "I texted Hunter's picture to a friend of mine who's a TA at Columbia."

Of course, she had a friend who could help. I swear Sandy knew everyone. She continued, "The Hunter who attended Columbia was a stocky redhead."

A convincing backstory disproven by luck and Sandy. "If Officer Richards' cousin didn't attend Columbia, where has he been for the past ten years?"

"I have no idea. Maybe the chief can find out," Sandy suggested.

Uncle G would leave no stone unturned. His mission to out fakes trumped mine. I still felt bad for Sandy, but better that she knew about the man now rather than later. As luck would have it, I spotted Russ's Land Rover parked beside Uncle G's vehicle as I left the Sit and Stay Café.

Head high, Champ power-walked beside me along Fifth Street toward police headquarters. One of the few all-brick structures in a town filled with airy, gingerbread-trimmed Victorians and iconic mansard roofs, the building's clean lines seemed appropriate for those who protected and served.

Inside, I caught Officer Richards scratching the back of his neck behind the granite reception desk. Forget pleasantries. "Are you okay?" Normally a towering force to be reckoned with, the redhead looked like he'd slept in a poison ivy patch. His foot-to-foot shift none too subtly brushed his back against the door frame, confirming his discomfort.

"Allergy," he explained.

"To what?" Empathy flooded me. I scratched mosquito bites until I bled.

"Peanuts." He reached across his chest to scratch his opposite shoulder. "I'm lucky it was only one shot."

"You drank it on purpose?" I asked.

"Not exactly. I won big last night at darts and drank my cousin Hunter's peanut butter whisky by mistake."

My "Ick!" slipped out. "That's a thing?"

"Yeah." He reversed his arms and scratched his other shoulder. "Didn't know until it was too late. Could've been worse. Last time I ended up in the ER. I didn't need the EpiPen last night."

"Have you seen the doc?"

"He gave me a prescription." Richie's grimace put his comfort level at a two. Champ sensed it as well. His sympathetic grunt made us both laugh.

The meds weren't working yet. I hated to ask, but... "Before he came to Barkview, when was the last time you saw your cousin?"

"A couple of years ago at a family reunion," Richie replied.

"Where did he go to school?"

"I don't remember." Richie's frown indicated he had more to say. "My cousin is..."

"Is what, Richie?" I tried for the right amount of schoolmarm sternness and confidence in my tone.

"It's nothing," Richie said unconvincingly.

"It's something." Whatever he added would be important. I knew it. "Kind of feels like he's not telling you everything. Huh?" I hated to put words in his mouth, but this was different. I got family loyalty. I really did. I'd lie under oath to protect my Aunt Char.

"Yeah." He nodded, relieved that I understood. "It's the way he asked me about Barkview's no-camera policy. He wanted to know how we patrolled without them."

My "I see" kept Richie talking. "I didn't think anything about it until he called the stadium a generational make-out spot."

Decades of iconic car styles came to mind, all parked in a drive-in lot. "It used to be a drive-in back in the day."

"That's the point. Hardly anyone knows that. Hunter hated history. Why would he look up stuff on Barkview?" Richie asked.

Another anomaly on the Hunter Richards list. I pointed toward the chief's closed office door. "Russ in with the chief?"

"Yeah. Knock before you go in."

With a breezy "Feel better," I headed toward Uncle G's glass-walled office, hesitating when I saw the blinds were closed. Champ's single bark acted like a knock.

"Enter." Uncle G's bellow almost made me turn tail. I probably would have if the bat dog hadn't nosed the dog door open. He ripped the leash from my hand and bounded inside. Champ greeted Russ with crazy tail wags and happy wiggles. Like it or not, I followed. If only I felt as secure.

Flanked by deputy dogs Max and Maxine, Uncle G sat

behind his smoked-glass desk. Autographed photos of two previous presidents shaking his hand hung on the gray wall behind him, a testament to a career well spent. A fancy TV screen overwhelmed the only other non-glass wall.

"This better be good," he growled. Between the toothpick twirling in his mouth and the wrinkles in his rolled-up cuffs that spoke of too many hours since he'd reported in this morning, he had intimidation covered.

Despite having Richie's permission to enter, I wasn't immune either.

"Hunter Richards is a fraud. His degree from Columbia is a sham," I announced.

The chief's toothpick twirl stopped. "I see."

He didn't, not really, until I laid out my findings. In fact, Mel and Richie's info all came out in a rush. "He was at the stadium Wednesday around midnight... I think he's involved..." The pause went on for what felt like forever until Russ jumped in.

"The timing fits regarding the stolen Candy Catcher card," Russ suggested with knight-errant charm.

I thanked him with a smile. I liked having someone on my side. "Hunter has been watching Austin Bruns, who has made it no secret he wants the card." Attaining it illegally didn't exactly fit the man's plan, but I was open to suggestions. Said out loud, all my suspicions added up to a whole lot of nothing.

"His drink caused Richie to end the dart game early last night," I added. "Will said he didn't return to his room until the morning shift came on."

Uncle G cleared his throat. "A good-looking guy like that? Not sure you want to know where he spent the night."

My cheeks burned. "I know I'm right. There's something off about Hunter."

Just then, Hunter strolled into the office. "You have excellent instincts, Mrs. Hawl. I would appreciate it if you would keep them to yourself."

Both German Shepherds stood at attention. Champ scooted between us. Up close, Hunter really was shockingly good-looking in a bad-boy kind of way. One look into those promising sapphire-blue eyes, and I was caught.

"I apologize for interrupting. Richie told me to come in. Allow me to introduce myself. Hunter Richards, SSCCTF." He flashed a badge.

I flopped into the nearest desk chair. Relief mixed with excitement for Sandy. Hunter was one of the good guys. "What is SSCCTF?" I really hated acronyms.

"Secret Service Cryptocurrency Task Force," Hunter said. "I am in Barkview investigating cryptocurrency fraud."

Yeah. Sandy suited this guy too well.

"My background was airtight. How did you see through it, Mrs. Hawl?" he asked.

"Sandy figured it out," I replied. "Call me Cat." Russ's mother was Mrs. Hawl. "What were you doing at the stadium?"

"Surveillance. We've traced the currency transfers to small towns like Barkview during and directly following baseball memorabilia events."

The legal transfer of assets. Uncle G rose to his unmovable lumberjack stance. "Why wasn't I informed?"

"The MO is a local agent or distributor," Hunter replied.

All the more reason to advise Uncle G. Unless the Secret Service thought he could be involved. Uncle G's growl confirmed our conclusions matched.

"Why did you come forward now?" I asked quickly.

"Sandy's inquiry alerted my team. Her research technique is the best I've encountered. Blew an eighteen-month under-cover investigation."

Begrudging approval? She'd impressed him. I liked the possibilities.

"What made you suspect I wasn't who I claimed to be?" he asked.

"Mel Witman."

"Ah, her not-so-out-of-left-field baseball card question." He shook his head. "Seems suspicion runs in Barkview."

"Only for newbies." Not that Barkviewian locals didn't have secrets. We just ignored them on a daily basis.

"Even those with family ties?" Hunter asked.

"Especially when they poison one of ours," I shot back, glad we'd blown the perfect setup wide open.

"I drink peanut butter whiskey. Richie shooting mine was bad luck." Hunter glanced at his watch. Was he in a rush? "I'll explain what I can." He faced Uncle G. "Maybe you can offer insights."

I was all ears until my smart watch alarm went off. Not another Champ event. Sure enough, an appearance at the Barkview Hospital started in fifteen minutes. I didn't dare miss it. Champ's owner, Michael, had requested it, no doubt to check up on me and his celebrity dog. One look at Hunter's grin, and I knew he'd timed his arrival perfectly. A need-to-know conversation couldn't include me anyway. If Hunter expected Russ to fill me in behind the scenes, he'd be disappointed. My husband kept confidences better than Area 51. That was our biggest marital issue. No, not our issue—mine. I'd known the need-to-know nature of his business before I married him.

I rose slowly. I knew when I'd been beaten. "Come, Champ." The bat dog fell in beside me.

"I trust my secret is safe with you, Cat," Hunter said.

I wanted to add conditions but only nodded. I'd been tasked with finding the missing Candy Catcher card. "I do have a question that shouldn't compromise your position." He inclined his head. "On Wednesday night, who did you see at the stadium?"

"Other than Mel Witman?" Hunter asked.

Hunter neatly turned that around. Uncle G's frown promised retribution. So be it. A reporter never gave up their sources.

"Touché. I'm serious. Did you see anyone else?" I asked.

"Why do you need to know?" Hunter asked.

"Sweetheart, you don't want to be late." Russ's interference stopped my response. For some reason, he didn't want me admitting that the Candy Catcher baseball card was missing.

I heeded his warning. There was more going on here than Hunter had admitted. This case was becoming more complicated at every turn. What part did the Fab Five and the missing baseball card play?

CHAPTER 15

In the dog-friendliest city in America, a "no dogs allowed" policy at the Barkview Hospital ought to be illegal. People connected with dogs. Even I understood that. Why the hospital administrators refused to allow canine visitation made me crazy. Sure, maintaining a sterile environment played a big part in full recovery, but so did mental health. I had to wonder how many people disobeyed. I'd even snuck Renny in for a therapeutic visit to see Aunt Char during her last stay.

Today I thumbed my nose at the sign as Champ and I bypassed the reception desk and walked through the comfortable lobby en route to the tropical atrium. Patients gowned in blue dolphin-printed robes, colorfully dressed nurses, and plainclothes visitors greeted us as we entered the lush paradise. Glassed on three sides, with a babbling water feature meandering through tropical foliage spotted with colorful orchids and bromeliads, the space offered a serene healing environment. My blood pressure eased every time I entered.

Champ liked it too. After a curious sniff, he got right to work. He charmed everyone there, signing paw-o-graphs, posing for selfies, and enjoying group pets. The patients' happy smiles and phrases strengthened my will to fight the dog rule yet again.

"Remind me not to get on your bad side." RJ Ruff's deep voice made me jump. Not that he'd scared me—I'd been so focused on Champ that he'd simply surprised me. RJ Ruff wasn't an intimidating man. In fact, the phrase "average Joe" came to mind. A man of medium height and weight with light brown hair and unmemorable eyes, he looked familiar in an undefinable way.

"I'm not that scary." I couldn't believe my good fortune running into him.

"You are formidable," he replied.

Was that a compliment? I wasn't sure.

RJ's chuckle indicated it was. "You're right. The no-dogs rule is shortsighted and ridiculous in this town. I pity the hospital board when you are done with them."

That he'd read my mind reinforced my need to better mask my feelings. "It makes no sense," I muttered. Champ materialized at my side and offered RJ his paw.

The man smiled and met him halfway. "Not every day a celebrity wants to shake my hand."

I doubted that. RJ's nonthreatening manner made him approachable. No wonder he did so well in the chaotic sports memorabilia world.

"Are you here visiting someone?" I asked.

"I suppose I am."

An evasive or just odd answer? He wore no hospital ID band.

"Would you mind signing a Champ baseball card for me?" he asked.

"Really? They aren't collectible." RJ's baseball memorabilia collection was reportedly first class.

"Perhaps someday they will be. I collect originals. The first bat dog in the major leagues will be a classic."

Assuming Champ was that dog. I took his request as the compliment he'd intended and placed the card beside Champ's paw. The bat dog stepped on the ink pad and signed the card. I offered it to RJ with a caramel.

RJ waved off the candy. "Thank you. I look forward to the Candy Catcher exhibit opening. The card's artwork is baseball's equivalent of the *Mona Lisa*."

High praise from an expert. "And their batting record still stands."

"It will likely stand for a long time. Five teammates hitting over .500 is a statistical impossibility."

I figured as much. "How'd they do it?"

"They cheated." He said it so matter-of-factly it took me a second to process it.

"Cheated? You can't be serious." But he was. Not even a flicker in his expression proved it. Was he calling out Bark U's most honored sportsmen?

"But I am. Some say it was luck. Others, magic. They dipped the bat's knob and handle in caramel."

Because everyone wanted burned sugar and butter on their hands. I wiggled my right fingers, imagining the sticky goo. "Doesn't soaking a bat in pine tar do the same thing?" Champ had been trained to ignore the smell. I wondered if he would've preferred the sugary mix.

"According to 1952 rules, you are correct." RJ's affable smile returned. "The ants certainly liked it."

Now that was a vision. It also brought up a question about what really happened in the caramel factory the night of the fire. "Do you think the original Fab Five cards still exist?"

RJ readjusted the embroidered Barkers Baseball windbreaker draped across his arm. "There have been many offers, but no recorded sales in seventy years."

"Not that you'd admit to." I watched for a reaction. I'd all but called him a liar.

His expression remained unchanged. "Your husband asked me the same question. I will tell you what I told him. I am an expert on the Fab Five Hundred, and I have only authenticated the Candy Catcher card." On that note, he exited.

I didn't stop him. Champ's tail suddenly beat against my calf. Before I could complain, the dog abandoned me and ran to his owner's wheelchair. The bat dog didn't excitedly jump into Michael's arms. Instead, he licked his hand below the IV and dropped his head onto Michael's leg.

No jealousy on my part. Well, maybe a little. The reunion renewed my belief that a special bond existed between the right dog and owner. While Champ effectively did his job under my care, I swear he came to life in Michael's presence.

"The doctor says I'll be out of here in a day or two." Pale as a freshly bleached sheet, I hoped Michael looked better than he had when admitted two days ago. "My wife arrives tomorrow in time for the Candy Catcher card reveal."

If there was one. The clock was ticking. "You have a baseball card collection, right?" I waited for his nod. "Why would a collector want to acquire a card anonymously? Isn't showing them off why you do it?"

"I'm no psychiatrist, but..." He cringed as he tried to get more comfortable in the seat. "I share my cards with my kids. I want them to love the game as much as I do. Some people are just about the collecting."

No great revelations there.

"We'll get Champ off your hands soon," Michael said.

"No rush. He's a pleasure. I'm enjoying working with him." Champ butt-bumped my leg in agreement. I really did, I realized. Champ loved Russ too. If only the allergies weren't an issue.

Michael's chuckle ended in a cough.

"Aunt Char insists both you and Melissa stay with her until you are ready to travel." I stopped his protest. "I suggest you save your energy and agree now. My aunt will not be denied."

"You two know how to coerce a man when he's down." Michael stroked Champ's back in thoughtful contemplation.

"We'd also like you to consider opening a training center in Barkview."

My invitation drew a tired smile. "You offering to be my first customer?"

"I... No. I don't own a..." I sputtered.

"I'm just teasing you, Cat." His joke ended in another cough.

That I wasn't violently opposed to having a dog in my life surprised me. Me, adopt a dog? I couldn't think about it now.

Michael's yawn indicated it was time for us to leave.

"You be a good boy and go with Cat." Champ's sidelong look questioned the command, but his work ethic allowed nothing else. Despite feeling to the contrary, the bat dog stoically followed me out of the building, looking back a handful of times until he jumped into my SUV.

I was a poor second. "It'll be over soon. I promise." I rubbed Champ's ears. He sighed in his doggie way that stirred guilt.

I felt for him. I really did. Being separated from the one you love was no fun. If anyone came between Russ and me... I wouldn't be as understanding.

I headed home, visions of my fluffy robe and slippers on my mind. I got as far as First Street before Sandy texted, requesting that I meet her and Jennifer at the baseball card museum. So much for a quiet evening at home.

I left Russ a message detailing the change of plans as I

drove past the Old Barkview Inn and turned east on Willow. I doubted he'd beat me home, but no sense worrying him if I was delayed.

A few minutes later, I drove into the museum's parking lot and parked beside Sandy's Jeep by the blue awning. Had it only been thirty hours since the Candy Catcher card had gone missing? It felt like forever.

Sandy opened the passenger door for Champ.

"Planning on jumping?" I asked. The bulging backpack slung over her shoulder had to be a parachute.

Sandy's giggle sounded promising. "Just being prepared for anything. Which reminds me. You should change your shoes."

Kitten heels served many purposes. Looking for hidden rooms in a dusty stadium probably wasn't on that list. I popped the back hatch. Since my pickleball bag served as my dash bag, the wardrobe change took no time.

"You're prepared for anything?" I asked.

"Anything. I have water, protein bars, a charging station, Champ's fetching bat, treats, and flares."

I bit back a laugh. Everyone needed a battery-charging station on an adventure. Had to admire her earnestness. Time for the don't-overthink-it lesson. "Where's Amanda?" Surely, she was part of this adventure. We needed her keys to access the building. I couldn't believe I had beaten her anywhere. The woman rivaled FedEx for on-time arrival.

"No. Jennifer took her to dinner tonight." Sandy's sapphire-blue eyes twinkled.

Inclusive Sandy keeping Amanda busy elsewhere did not bode well. "Do I want to know?" A rhetorical question, for sure. Of course, I wanted—no, needed—to know.

Sandy blurted it out. "Sully never left Vegas because he was a wannabe magician/illusionist."

Her pause drew me right in. "So."

"He had his own act, which never made it to the Strip. He did help create tricks for fellow illusionists in the 1960s and 1970s. He also created some amazing puzzle boxes, too. The tributes to his work from his funeral are cool."

"What does that mean?" Illusionists relied on misdirection and what the audience thought they saw versus what they really saw.

"I think the secret door isn't really where you think it is." Sandy's bubbling excitement confused me more than it enlightened.

"The crack in the concrete is on the museum wall," I explained.

"A misdirect. You're thinking too linearly. If not through the wall, then..."

The light clicked on. "Under it. A tunnel." Of course. It made way too much sense in Barkview and explained why no one found it during the building's remodels.

"Jennifer found this." The gaslight's glare on Sandy's tablet required me to shade it with my palm to read it. "It's the renovation plan from 1982." Sandy pointed to the stairwell. "That has to be it."

A denotation for an air duct under the stairwell in the floor? Worth investigating. I glanced at the locked museum door. "I hate to be a buzzkill, but how do we get inside without Amanda?" A B&E on Uncle G's watch would be one thing, but with Hunter Richards and the Secret Service involved? Federal jurisdiction added a whole new dimension.

"The same way all those girls snuck in over the years." No missing Sandy's kid-in-the-candy-store smile. She had a plan —one I doubted I'd like.

"Great. We get to take the walk of shame," I remarked. "For the record, why isn't Amanda here? She'll be thrilled the 'secret door' mystery has been solved."

Had to love Sandy's expressive responses; I always knew what she was thinking. She sobered instantly. "Illusionists have assistants."

That bad feeling pooled in my stomach. I knew where this was going. "Amanda's mother?"

"And aunt. Amanda had to have at least suspected about the tunnel."

Denial sprang to mind. "Amanda admitted to looking for it but claimed to have never found it."

"You might be too close to this one," Sandy said matter-of-factly.

Maybe I was. I genuinely wanted to believe Amanda hadn't found the secret door. We'd both arrived in Barkview about the same time and shared Barkview's newbie initiation. An oversight, or another Barkview secret to unravel?

Sandy said nothing, waiting on my next move.

"Lead on," I said finally. Only finding the truth would answer my questions. The first step was to find the entry and see if it revealed additional clues.

Sandy switched on her phone light.

"Seriously? You didn't bring a flashlight?"

She looked at me like I was crazy. "Use your phone."

"My phone." The glowing screen about blinded me.

Sandy stepped up and turned on the flashlight feature. "Let's go."

I followed. I shivered in the cool, overcast evening air and followed her into the inky darkness toward the right-field wall. Note to self: a silk blouse and light blazer didn't offer adequate warmth for coastal spring evenings.

Built in three-foot textured-stucco sections, the wall with its mural blended into the craggy hillside and appeared to be an extension of the Barkview Cliffs.

"The drive-in concession stand was just about here back in

the day." Sandy referred to her tablet and counted twenty paces from the building's corner. She paused at the first section's seam and ran her fingers down the opening. "If Jennifer's calculations are correct, there's a door around here."

"Here?" I'd learned not to question Jennifer's research, but an entrance behind the right-field home-run fence required any visitors to travel the length of the open field to get to the "secret room."

"In 1952 the museum area was part of the home team's locker room," Sandy pointed out. "The remodel opened up more space between the wall and current entry."

I didn't argue further. The location still made no sense. I focused my light on the next panel seam. "What am I looking for?"

"A latch."

How hard could that be to find? I reached under the stucco and immediately yanked my hand back. "Ick!" I shook off the creepy-crawly cobwebs and who knew what else resided under there.

"Seriously?" I ignored Sandy's eye roll. I hated spiders almost as much as snakes. No way I'd do that again.

Champ saved me. The dog sniffed with Bloodhound diligence along the base of the wall. He stopped three sections beyond Sandy and pawed at the panel.

Sandy abandoned her location to investigate. Her bare fingers ran the length of the seam. A bursting-helium-balloon pop broke the stillness. The wall swung about twelve inches inward.

"Come on." Without a backward glance, Sandy slipped through the opening. Champ wiggled in behind her before I could even verbalize an objection.

Warning bells went off. Russ was going to have my head for this. Not that he ruled my life, but a thief and potential cybercriminal operating in Barkview made sneaking around not only foolish, but potentially hazardous. If we backed off now...we hadn't done anything prosecution-worthy yet.

Me, think about consequences on a quest? Was it intuition or guilt? I'd fearlessly broken into an Indian casino in search of information on the Howard Looc case. That was before I'd married Russ. Before I'd become a community leader. Before responsibility became a daily thing. Was I becoming my Aunt Char?

That realization scared me more than my fear of criminals. I squashed my warring conscience. I turned sideways, sucked in my breath, and slipped into the stadium. The door magically clicked shut behind me. That wasn't creepy or anything.

I knee-bumped Champ who stood just outside Sandy's light beam. The dog pressed into my thigh.

"What happened? Did you see someone?" Sandy's breathlessness indicated she'd backtracked for me.

No way I could explain that little confidence crisis. "No. I'm in." All-in now, for better or worse, despite the chilling foreboding. Where Champ went, I followed. With any luck the presiding judge would be a Labrador fan.

Her tablet in treasure-map-referral position, Sandy signaled for me to follow her. Champ fell in right behind Sandy. With a no-turning-back-now look at the exit, I brought up the rear.

Our jog down the right-field line and past the dugout took less than two minutes. Long enough to get caught if someone watched, but easy enough if a third-party lookout distracted any would-be reporters. I made a mental note to follow up on that possibility.

Tonight, we entered the dark players' entrance area without incident. From the field, the stairwell leading to the second-floor coach's observation area and box seats was to the left. The Barkview Barkers' locker room entrance on the right begged a peek.

I tapped Sandy's shoulder. I'd heard too much about that locker room not to look. Sandy chuckled and followed me inside.

I'm not sure what I expected behind those hallowed walls, but a sweaty jock hangout that fell well short of the Barkview Racquet Club's changing-room standards wasn't it. Rows of full-length metal lockers fronted with wooden benches lined the main room. The white subway-tiled shower area and therapy pool had a timeless good-old-boy feel that made me wonder if this locker room had measurably changed since the Fab Five's day.

Detour completed, we returned to the stairwell. Champ pawed at the wall where he'd discovered the crack. I observed from the doorway. Not that I'd criticize Sandy's plan. I hoped I'd think of something as a result of her efforts.

Sandy referred to her tablet. I watched her grid-pattern examination of the floor tiles surrounding the floor vent. No hollow sound when stomped on. No odd movement.

"It can't be that easy. Someone would've found it years ago." I leaned back against the staircase wall. My heel caught as if superglued to something, twisting my ankle as I tried to break free. Recovery impossible, I went down like a stately Torrey Pine, cracking the back of my head on the stairwell wall.

Champ jumped over to me and licked my face. Ick! Why did he think that helped?

"Are you okay?" Sandy's concern came through the haze. How hard had I hit my head?

"Yeah. My foot stuck. I twisted my ankle..." I waved off her offered hand up, investigating instead. I found the round disk-like indentation by running my fingertips over the floor. The tiles blended so well I could hardly see it, even up close. "Can you shine a light here?"

Sandy knelt beside me and focused her cellphone light on it. "Wow! That hole's too cylindrical to be accidental."

My pulse jumped. It looked like a keyhole of sorts. "What props did Sully use most in his acts?"

"Balls and bats for his baseball tricks."

A single-minded individual. The hole was too small for a baseball to fit, but the handle of a bat... "The Fab Five were the all-time best hitters. You have Champ's fetching bat in there?"

"Yeah." Sandy swung her backpack around and removed the mini-bat. "It's the standard grip size."

I placed the handle into the hole. It fit perfectly. I turned it right. Nothing.

"Try left. Sully was left-handed." Her bubbling excitement rubbed off.

The bat turned. I think I expected something like a jack-in-the-box to jump out, to reward us for finding it. When nothing happened, I twisted it again, harder this time. "Come on." Sheer determination prevailed. The wall beneath the staircase swung open.

CHAPTER 16

Sandy aimed her light into the room under the staircase. Sure, there was dust, but the footprints weren't seventy years old. Someone had been in here recently. With further scrutiny, I identified the distorted shapes as the frame of a camp chair, its material eaten by time, two World War II–era can-shaped lights, a bat rack, and a lantern.

"This can't be the rendezvous room," I said. "It's too small for a bed."

Sandy crawled inside, brushing dust aside with a towel she'd magically removed from her backpack. "Sully worked a lot with trapdoors. This may be a... Sweet!!"

The creak of old wood revealed a hole in the floor. Champ lunged toward it, only to back up in retreat. I saw it then: a rope ladder with wood planks for steps dangling against the rock wall, descending into an abyss.

I gulped, my imagination running wild. "Where does it go?"

"It should lead to the museum."

"Though it could only be a fallout shelter. They were a

thing in the 1950s and 1960s." Sandy shrugged. "Or a part of an old Prohibition-era smuggling tunnel like we found on the north side of town. We'll need to look to be sure."

Not more tunnels. I shivered at that possibility. "Let's know for sure before we speculate."

A tunnel would explain why the secret room had never been found.

Sandy shone her light into the hole. "It looks safe enough. Come on. Let's find out." She started to descend.

"Wait, Sandy..." Too late. Her blonde ponytail vanished into the darkness.

A second later, Sandy's voice echoed from below. "Wow! This is cool. You need to see this."

"Hang on. I need to call..." I fumbled for my phone, dropping it into the black hole thanks to Champ head-bumping my arm. Not that I blamed him. The dog instinctively wanted to follow, but a swinging pirate's rope-ladder wasn't exactly dog-friendly.

Instinct called for instant pursuit, but did I dare leave Champ? I trusted him to stay where commanded. I flexed my fingers. Did I have a choice?

I still hesitated. Was it intuition or just plain fear? My last tunnel adventure had nearly cost me my life.

"It's not that deep. Champ can stand guard," Sandy called.

I squinted. She was right. The cylindrical hole didn't appear too deep. Maybe ten or twelve feet. And Russ did know we were at the stadium...

"I dropped my phone." Although hardly above a whisper, I swear my voice echoed. It wasn't like anyone else was around, but sneaking around made me nervous. Light flickered below me.

"Yeah. I have it." Her phone light beam illuminated the

space directly below. "You really need to see this." Sandy's reply had just enough awe to trigger my curiosity.

Forget trepidation, I was all in. "I'm coming. Champ. Sit. Stay." The dog whined. He didn't want to obey, but good training prevailed. The dog gave me the you're-insane look and plopped down beside the trapdoor.

Maybe I was. Getting a grip on the unsteady rope-ladder took a minute. Adjusting to the ladder's sway took another. It wasn't like I was a total klutz; the rope wasn't even. One side hung lower than the other. A vision of girls in poofy poodle skirts and saddle shoes climbing down this ladder for a rendezvous made me laugh. Was I ever glad I wore court shoes now.

Three rungs down, the smell of stale, musty air struck me. I held on with one hand, the natural rock edges scraping my knuckles as I looked over my shoulder. Sandy's light about blinded me.

"Be careful. The rope's a little unsteady," she said.

My arms would feel the climb back up for sure. Hand under hand, I descended three more rungs. A coolness wrapped around me. My neck hairs tingled. Was Sandy right? Did this hole have another exit?

My Google Pixel Watch pinged with Russ's number. Perfect timing. He'd want to know about the tunnel. Probably not the smartest move, but with one hand holding on to the ladder rung, I swiped across my watch face with the other and spoke into my watch. "Hi, Russ. We found the tunnel." The line crackled and went dead. How much had he heard?

"Don't you ever plug this in?" I deserved Sandy's exasperation. In all fairness, it was the end of the day, and I typically recharged overnight.

Her light bounced up, down, and all around the darkness for a second and then refocused on me. At the same time, the trap door snapped shut above, and the right side of the rope ladder jerked. My stomach bottomed out. Never good in an emergency, I screamed. I couldn't help it. Not that anyone could hear me over Champ's insistent barking.

Oddly, I did hear Sandy's "Uh-oh," or was it just fortuitous that I looked upward at that moment? I'd expected Hollywood-style frayed ropes hanging on by a single strand and straining to hold my considerable weight, not the rope hanging from a loose metal ring dangling drunkenly from the rock.

Instinct sent me scrambling upward. Not the right move. My panicked movement did it. The metal fitting popped out of the rock wall, causing the ladder to collapse. I swear, I relived every terrifying roller-coaster drop-off as I plunged to the ground.

Not far, it turned out. I landed on Sandy. I'm not sure if she tried to catch me or just didn't get out of the way fast enough, but we both hit the dirt. I tasted dust a second after my right shoulder jammed into the ground.

Sandy's groan made it sound like she'd ended up on her back. I couldn't tell for sure. The second I hit Sandy, the room had plunged into total, disorienting darkness. Only the sound of Champ's barking indicated which way was up.

"Are you okay?" I asked after a quick physical inventory.

"Yeah. I dropped both phones. Feel around. They can't be far." No panic in Sandy's voice, just let's-get-the-job-done determination.

I rolled to my knees. The crackle and crunch could only mean one thing. "I found one." Let's hope it was my powerless phone. I'd really killed it this time.

It was. A moment later, Sandy's light clicked on, and I saw this underground walk-in closet for the first time. Part excavated tunnel and part natural rock, the room reminded me of the Prohibition smugglers' tunnels I'd found on the north side of town, except this one had been closed off. Two walls appeared to be original, and fallen rock made up the remaining two. A casualty of the many California earthquakes or a forgotten World War II bomb shelter? Either way, the Candy Catcher must've told Sully about it. How else could he have found it?

The Fab Five had converted the cave into a boys' clubhouse, complete with the iconic white swimsuit pinup of Betty Grable's million-dollar legs and a poster of Brigitte Bardot. Five faded plastic chairs were pushed up against a card table in front of the only bare wall. I noted the trapdoor above it. No doubt back in 1952 it provided access into the famous secret room. Obviously, a ladder had been there. Had it fallen in disrepair, or had someone removed it?

"How are we going to get out of here?" Sandy asked.

Good question. I expected optimism and determination, not what-do-we-do-now uncertainty from my number-one cheerleader. "Not the way we got in," I replied. Without the ladder, there was no way we'd climb the smooth rock walls leading to the hole we'd climbed down through.

My flippant comment worked. Sandy laughed. "You're sure about that?"

"Pretty sure." I squeezed her shoulder. "Let's start by searching the room. There could be another way out."

Sandy's brain clicked into action. "Wait a minute." She examined her cell phone. "No signal." She tried every corner, even standing on one of the chairs in search of the elusive signal. "Still nothing. Turn yours on."

"Mine? Why would mine work and not yours?" That made no sense. We used the same cell carrier.

I obeyed her just-do-it look even before she explained, "Just because you can't make a call doesn't mean the location tracking doesn't work. That means Russ might still be able to find you."

My husband having 24/7 eyes on me wasn't a particularly pleasant thought. Today, though, I rather hoped he did.

I plugged my phone into the power. To think I'd thought this was a dumb thing to bring on our adventure. My cellphone dinged when the power went on and scrolled through the standard welcome sequence. No service bars appeared.

Technological solutions exhausted, Sandy handed me a chocolate-covered power bar. "Everything looks better covered in chocolate. Right?"

A great rule to live by. I savored the dark chocolate coating, thinking about Sully. Why hadn't he left a personal item? Or had he? It would be something more subtle. "Look for a hidden panel. Something Sullyish," I said.

With Sandy's phone light on high power, we searched every nook on the rocky walls. Nothing. I was missing something. I could feel it.

I inventoried the room's contents on Post-its and laid them out on the table with my other notes. My Post-its didn't stick so well to the dust-covered table, but the visuals helped organize my thoughts. "Where did they put their bats?"

"Bats?" Sandy must've thought I'd lost my mind.

"Bats," I repeated.

"I guess they left them in the bat rack by the trapdoor up there?" She pointed skyward. "The rope ladder wasn't stable enough to bring them down here."

It sounded all wrong. "A bunch of twenty-year-old athletes who happened to be world-record hitters? I bet those guys slept with their bats." I let my words sink in.

I watched Sandy's excitement build. "They would be hidden someplace special."

"With a secret lock. Sully liked those," I suggested.

"He also liked puzzles," Sandy reminded me. Like a bloodhound on a fresh scent, she reexamined the main wall, angling the phone light to throw shadows against the surface. "Got something! It is a roundish hole, hidden beneath a mirror. Hand me the mini-bat."

I did. Sandy inserted the knob and turned the barrel. The click released an ingenious sliding door. Cell light directed into the hidden cabinet revealed five bats, each signed by its Fab Five owner, hung in an intricately carved display.

Sandy whistled. "Wow! These have to be worth a fortune."

No kidding. I fingered the Candy Catcher bat. The manufacturer's markings matched those of the bat in the Fab Five's museum display. "If this is the Candy Catcher's actual bat, then whose is in the museum's display?" How had Amanda been fooled? My intuition waved a red flag. "Let's lock this back up for now."

"Fine. Amanda can figure that out later." Sandy relocked the cabinet. That my curious assistant hadn't asked why should've prepared me for her next bombshell. "We have a bigger problem."

"Bigger than being locked in a subterranean room?" I wiped tears from my burning eyes. The churned-up dust was getting worse.

"Yeah. We need to conserve. The ventilation in here isn't great." She coughed to prove it. "I bet it hasn't been serviced in a long time."

"But..." The door we'd climbed down through had closed when the rope ladder fell. "We're really locked in, aren't we?"

Sandy nodded. "I can't hear Champ barking any more. Do you think he went for help?"

I nodded. "Of course he did. You know how amazing that dog is." I had to believe it. "All we can do is wait." Beneath my optimism, real fear stirred.

"Yeah. I don't want to scare you, but based on size, this room has roughly a thousand cubic feet of air. If we stay calm, we breathe nineteen or so cubic feet of air an hour. That means we have about a day and a half of air in here."

I hated it when she got all mathematical on me. I felt my airways tightening. I would have cried if Sandy hadn't needed me to remain calm and positive. "I'll starve to death before then."

"Not for a while. You can live for weeks without food. No water will get you in a few days." Sandy pulled two water bottles out of her backpack.

"You're amazing. You knew that without the internet."

Her grin seemed bittersweet. "We'll lose the lights first. Between both phones and the charging station, we might have twelve hours."

Basically, until morning. Not that we could tell when that would be with no windows.

"I-I don't like the dark." Sandy's voice cracked.

Neither did I. My stomach clenched just thinking about it. "Russ will find us." I meant it. "He won't stop until he does." My husband promised to protect me. He never broke his word.

"I know, but we need to be realistic. We're ten feet underground. He could be standing over our heads, and we'd never even know he was there."

True, but... "Champ knows where we are." I hugged Sandy tight. "We'll get through this together. Let's try to get some sleep."

I switched off my light. Only the glow from Sandy's phone illuminated the chamber. This was going to be a long night.

CHAPTER 17

I woke with a start, my heart racing, breathing like I'd run a mile. Something was coming for me!

It took a full minute for my eyes to adjust to the gloom and realize that I'd been dreaming. No lioness prowled at the door; the noise came from above.

"Sandy, are you awake?" I whispered. She stirred. "I hear something."

Sandy jumped to her feet, her phone light steadily increasing in wattage. "I do too." Despite our restless night, Sandy looked and moved like a teenager. I unfolded more gingerly, favoring my knee as I bent and stretched to work out the stiffness.

"We're down here. Can you hear me?" Sandy shouted. No response agitated her further. "We need to make noise."

"Do you know Morse code?" That was the most efficient way to send an SOS.

"Sure. Just give me..." Sandy tapped on her phone and then groaned. "Never mind. How do you do anything without the internet?"

No explaining to a millennial how we'd all managed to thrive before 1990-something. I picked up the mini-bat and tapped a rhythm on the rock wall beneath the trapdoor. I might not know Morse Code, but I knew the beat to songs—Russ's favorite, to be exact. And it worked. He tapped back the second chorus. Even Sandy recognized it. No missing the pounding above us or the dirt falling from the ceiling. Russ had some heavy equipment at work. Hopefully he wouldn't collapse the ground in his effort to get to us.

An hour later, just as my phone light flickered its almost-over warning, light flooded in through the hatch we'd climbed down through.

"Cat. Sandy. Are you all right?" Russ's concerned voice felt like a welcome home.

"Yes! Yes!" we shouted in unison. Champ's bark made it even better.

"Hunter's team found Champ in the parking lot. I'm now a big fan of all the doggie doors in Barkview," Russ explained.

Me too. Another Barkview regulation I'd come to respect.

"Champ led us to you. It took a while to figure out what his pawing meant," Russ admitted.

Relief coursed through me. He'd been there all along. Deep down I'd known it. "I'm impressed you figured out the door opened with the bat."

His "Oh" made me laugh. "How did you get the lock open?" I asked.

"I had the hole filled with resin, to create a key."

Practical, get-the-job-done Russ at his best. I glanced skyward in apology. Sully had to be furious. "It worked," I said.

"It didn't," Russ admitted. "The ground-penetrating radar and a sledgehammer finally opened it up."

He'd dropped an A-bomb on an anthill. Sully's seventy-year-old design had prevailed. I didn't want to think about Russ's frustration level during that process.

"The ladder will be here shortly," Russ said. "Step back. Here's some water."

An orange emergency pack plopped on the floor, sending up a puff of dirt. We both coughed. Sandy reacted first and opened the bag. The drink tasted good. So did the protein bars, even if they weren't chocolate-covered.

After taking a minute to relax, I noticed Sandy's stink-eye. "Hunter's team found Champ?" She waited for my nod. "You knew? When were you going to tell me that Hunter was one of the good guys?"

As if this was somehow my fault. "For the record, I tried to last night, but you dropped into this room before I could. After-ward..." My excuse sounded weak even to me.

"You had all night to tell me," Sandy insisted.

She'd had boyfriends before, but her flush said this guy was different. "Point taken. You didn't seem really interested in him." Or maybe I hadn't wanted to see it. Indecision hit hard. "I promised not to..."

"I will tell her myself." Hunter's words came as a gift from above, along with a telescoping silver ladder that unfolded like magical steps.

Before we could start our climb, Russ, and then Hunter, descended. As much as I enjoyed watching my husband's butt coming toward me, a bathroom seemed more important.

"What time is it?" I asked.

One hand on the ladder, Russ referred to his watch. "6:30."

"In the morning?" No way. I was awake without coffee. No light reference changed perception.

"I knew you could do it." He touched ground and wrapped me in a rib-crushing hug that muffled my retort. No sense bringing it up again. Hunter stood in front of Sandy.

"Shall we start again?" he asked.

Hunter waited for her nod before extending his hand. "Hunter Richards, Secret Service, Cybersecurity, undercover in Barkview."

"Sandy Wynn, impressed." She appeared poised and professional, but I knew better. The pink tint on her cheeks wasn't cosmetic.

Russ saw it too. His arms still around me, he whispered for my ears only, "Your Watson is growing up."

"She deserves it." I meant it, though I still choked up. Change, the only constant in life, loomed.

Russ gestured around the room. "We know how the thief got into the museum to steal the Candy Catcher card."

I nodded. "In addition to Clark Sugarland, Amanda Manley and Austin Bruns have direct links to the Fab Five and could have known about the secret room."

"Twelve hours until the Candy Catcher card's unveiling. We'd best get started looking for the baseball card," Russ said.

The pressure hit me. "I need a shower." I felt like I'd been dragged through a desert dust storm.

Russ gestured toward the ladder. "I'm extremely disappointed you didn't come home last night." His silky tone got my attention.

"You missed me?" His banter always led to something good, but here and now? I smelled like my grandmother's dust-bunny.

"I assure you, you missed me more."

"Really?" It wasn't like Russ to drag something out like this.

"I have some information you'll find... uh...helpful."

This ought to be good. "Okay. Let's hear it."

"Commander Daniel Smith was assigned to the naval station in San Diego. He had one daughter. Mary Ann Smith married Lieutenant Daniel Woofman on May 5, 1952. Their son, Fletcher Woofman, was born on December 7,1952, at the naval hospital in Pearl Harbor."

It didn't take a mathematician to figure this one out. The Fab Five's first baseman, Owen, did have an heir–a son who'd played baseball for Bark U and a grandson who currently lived a mile from the Barkview stadium! Woof had also been onsite replacing a window when Ella had seen the intruder.

"Are you sure you want to shower first?" Russ asked.

"No time." I scampered up the ladder like a limber kitten chasing catnip. I had four suspects, all with different links to the missing baseball card. Was its theft strictly financial? The Candy Catcher's bat and Champ's necklace staged at the crime scene indicated a personal motive—the kind an unacknowledged grandson might feel.

Related or not? I had twelve hours to figure out who had taken the baseball card and why.

The clock was ticking.

CHAPTER 18

I ended up showering at the Barkview Racquet Club while Russ took Champ for a walk. I hated to waste time, but both Russ and Champ covering their noses when I got into the vehicle made a cleanup mandatory.

Task completed, I felt better. I doubted the fashion sense of my mix-and-matched wardrobe. The new navy Racquet Club shirt and pickleball zippered jacket looked country-club casual. Yesterday's dusty, hastily aired-out slacks were better than a wrinkled pickleball skirt with leggings. Barely.

Locating the Candy Catcher baseball card while maintaining Champ's busy appearance schedule required some serious multitasking. A visit to Danny Woofman's glass shop before Champ's event at the youth baseball game fit in the schedule.

Since Russ agreed to accompany me, he drove the six blocks north on Third Street to the Hounds Hardware, a favorite DIY store. Weekend honey-doers filled the surrounding parking spaces, causing Russ to drive around the block twice before finding a parking place. I said nothing about Champ's park-anywhere permit. No doubt he'd find it preferential and demand I pay the tickets. I, on the other hand, had been performing a public service. No need to get into that debate now. Some things my husband didn't need to know.

Russ took charge of Champ as we walked around the back of the busy fix-it store to a small craftsman-style garage identified by the FFB Windows and Glass sign. Once a fancy auto repair shop, the space had been converted into auto and window glass storage by Woof's father when he'd settled in Barkview back in the 1980s. Woof lived above the shop in quarters he'd added around the turn of the twenty-first century.

We found Woof in the parking lot, loading up his panel truck.

"Working on Saturday?" Russ asked.

"I keep telling the windshields to crack on Monday. Not working out too well." Woof grinned. "Just one today so far. I gave the guys the day off to ready the tailgating barbeques."

It was just like Woof to take the weekend shift on game day. That he was dressed in his father's old Barkers Baseball jersey and jeans told me where he'd be headed after this repair.

"The entire Hawl family contingent. I feel honored." His Chihuahua's growl undermined Woof's warm welcome. I stepped back. Couldn't help myself. Aggressive dogs, even pint-sized Chihuahuas, did that to me.

"Don't mind the princess. She needs to work on sharing." Woof scooped up the shivering mini-dog. The fawn-colored handful settled into the crook of his arm, alert and defensive. The incongruity of the large man and toy dog still struck me.

"What can I do for you?" Woof asked.

No guile in his manner. Was he an Oscar-worthy actor, or did he have no idea what was going on? "We know you're related to Owen Daniels, the Fab Five's first baseman." I dropped that bomb, watching for his reaction.

Woof nodded, denying nothing. "My grandma told my father Owen was his biological father after the man who raised him passed back in 2006."

"Your dad played for the Barkview Barkers in the 1970s." I shared the statement for Russ's benefit. Coincidences never sat well with him. I preferred to reserve judgment.

"Yeah. Fate, I guess. Dad said Barkview always felt like home. That's why he started the glass replacement business here," Woof added. "And his foul ball history. He never understood why his mother refused to visit Barkview."

Mary Ann Woofman must've lived in constant fear, protecting her secret. "Do you have the Owen baseball card?"

Woof nodded. "Dad found it in his mother's papers when she died."

This was some story. "How did the Candy Catcher know about your father?"

"Owen had a letter delivered to him after his death. I don't know how Owen knew about my dad. He attended every one of Dad's baseball games, though. Never spoke to him. The Candy Catcher gave my grandma a box of ticket stubs and photos of dad on the field."

"Owen attended your father's baseball games?" I asked.

Woof nodded. "Every one of them. He was a good man."

Suddenly, I got it. Owen had been a proud father, too honorable to interfere. I touched Russ's arm. Mary Ann had found two good men in her life.

"Karl delivered Owen's baseball card to your grandma after his death?" I asked.

Woof's confusion dialed up my doubt. "No. Karl wanted Owen's baseball bat. He apologized to her for ruining her life and swore he would preserve the Fab Five's legacy."

My intuition tingled. "Your grandma had Owen's original bat since 1952?" The one I'd found in the secret cabinet.

"Yes. That night after the accident, Owen told her to find a whole man. He gave her the baseball card and the bat and requested that she destroy both. Grandma did find a husband, a good man who was a good husband and father, but she kept the card and bat."

"Why?" Russ asked. "She obviously didn't want anyone to know about him."

I knew. I glanced at Russ. Owen had been the love of her life. Some things your heart can't be parted from. "What could Karl have possibly said to compel her to give up the bat?"

"I don't know. It must've been good, though. She gave him the bat," Woof admitted.

"You know about the home-run room," Russ stated.

Woof's flush confirmed it. "My dad discovered it when he played ball here."

"All those foul balls?" Apparently, Woof's dad had been a better placement hitter than anyone had known.

Woof's chuckle confirmed it. "Yeah. A little extreme in my book, but that was Dad."

"He must've had a hard time with the lock," Russ added.

"I don't think so. Sully had a thing about bats. He used them in most of his illusions," Woof replied. "The man was a lifelong baseball fanatic."

Woof did know the chamber's secret. Or one of them anyway. "What do the baseball cards reveal?" I thought I might as well ask.

"Dad claimed it was the Fab Five's hitting secret."

Russ whistled. "That would be worth a lot of money."

"Yeah. Some things are worth more than money." Woof meant it.

"Like your grandfather Owen's legacy?" I asked.

Woof stroked his Chihuahua, looking everywhere but at me.

I didn't want it to be true, but suddenly, I knew. "Why did you take the Candy Catcher card?"

Woof puffed up like a rink-ready prizefighter. "To protect it."

"Protect it? From whom?" Russ and I asked in unison.

"Someone has three of the five cards. I have the remaining two. Without them, the Fab Five's secret remains myth." Woof's knight-errant statement resonated. He was a man prepared to die for his beliefs.

"How do you know one buyer has all the other cards? I understand they were bought by anonymous buyers. It likely...could've... been multiple people." I corrected myself mid-statement.

"It's a single buyer." He touched his heart. "I can't explain it. I just know."

Who was I to argue with that? If Woof was right, possessing the baseball cards wasn't about collecting at all, but a plan to expose the Fab Five's secret—to destroy the legacy built by five talented young men.

Woof crossed his arms, pressing the Chihuahua even closer to his heart. "The cards are safe. I will return the Candy Catcher baseball card and permanently loan the Owen card to the museum when this anonymous buyer is found."

A simple plan executed out of love. I couldn't fault him. I even supported him. Trust my husband to ruin a poignant moment with facts.

"Your motivation doesn't change the fact that what you have done is illegal," Russ pointed out.

"Arrest me. Owen was an honorable man. I will not allow his memory to be tarnished or the baseball card compromised." Bully growled in little-dog agreement.

I admired Woof's motives and resolve. But given his motivation, the violent nature of the Candy Catcher's card theft seemed hard to understand. "Why did you use Karl Sugarland's bat to break the card's display case?"

"What? I didn't use a bat." I knew Woof's surprise wasn't feigned. "I'd never chance damaging the baseball card." He rubbed his shoulder. "I lifted the card out of the case with gloves on, put it in a leather pouch, and left."

"What did you do to your shoulder?" Russ asked. Trust my husband to hone in on an important detail.

"I have a bad rotator cuff. Hurt it lifting an F-150 windshield a couple of weeks ago. Hate to admit I need the youngsters' help."

I believed him. So did Russ. Woof couldn't have swung the bat with that shoulder. That meant someone else—someone who also knew about the hidden room—had also tried to steal the card. Fortunately for Barkview, Woof had gotten there first. He didn't deserve to be punished for this.

"Woof is just trying to protect Barkview," I insisted.

"It doesn't make his actions legal," Russ replied, unbending.

And technically correct. How did I convince my husband that the right-versus-wrong law enforcement approach didn't apply?

Woof didn't flinch, his determination unwavering. This wasn't going to end well for anyone if I didn't find a compromise. "If Woof returns the Candy Catcher baseball card and loans the Owen card to the museum, they won't press charges." I could make that happen. Amanda would be thrilled, and Russ's security company could protect both cards. A win-win for all.

"Woof, I think we'd all be happier if you transferred both

baseball cards to the Barkview Bank's vault." I had to find common ground.

"Already done. Where do you think I'd put them?" Woof asked.

Of course, they were safely locked in the Woofmans' family box. The secrets that vault kept still shocked me.

"I'm not releasing them until the anonymous collector is exposed and his motives revealed," Woof insisted.

I didn't blame him.

"The Candy Catcher card display opens in"—Russ checked his watch—"eight hours. What do you intend to do?"

The reminder increased my stress. I found the baseball card but couldn't reveal it yet. I faced Russ. "We have to find the anonymous buyer." His nod indicated agreement.

I breathed a sigh of relief. "All right, Woof. What do you know about the anonymous buyer?"

The likelihood of incarceration diminishing, Woof relaxed. "RJ Ruff's not talking, but he knows something."

"He is a memorabilia dealer," Russ interjected. "Anonymous buyers are common."

"He's also a collector," Woof added. "And you know how collectors are."

I did. Someone with a personal vendetta had staged the theft's crime scene. "RJ has no connection to Karl Sugarland or the Fab Five."

There were three people who did have a familial relationship and potentially knew about the secret room.

Time to see Austin Bruns, Amanda Manley, and Clark Sugarland again.

CHAPTER 19

Much as I wanted to continue the hunt for the anonymous baseball card bidder, Champ's appearance at this morning's youth baseball game came first. The Lab loved kids. It was the perfect warm up for tonight's big game.

Boy, was I glad we'd left my car at the museum while Russ drove. The number of SUVs and minivans parked around the Dogwood Park baseball diamond not only proved youth baseball's popularity, but also introduced me, the never-before-ten-a.m. pickleball player, to the eye-opening world of sunrise kids' sports.

Talk about a lifestyle change. Russ dropped Champ and me at the home plate entrance and drove two blocks to Police Headquarters to park. I think he did it to avoid negotiating the scrum of strollers, teetering toddlers and tag-playing preschoolers with the celebrity dog. Not that Champ minded. His jersey and baseball cap on, he needed no help focusing on his task. The children's excited screeches and warm hugs didn't bother him at all.

A walk that I'd expected to take mere minutes ended with

me running and Champ loping along beside me to home plate for his introductions. Parents and news media lined up along the backstop, angling for the perfect pose. Sandy stood center-fray, recording on behalf of KDOG as each uniformed player high-fived Champ.

That she hadn't abandoned me made me feel good until I saw Russ conferring with Hunter outside the chain-link dugout fence.

I refocused on the young players. Their mini uniforms looked adorable. Standing about four feet tall, some taller, others shorter, wearing stretchy white baseball pants and blue-striped, short-sleeved jerseys, the Barker Boys looked like mini major leaguers. No wonder parents rushed to take photos. This was one of those memorable moments.

The welcome line completed, Champ and I stood between the visitors' dugout and home plate, waiting for the first bat to retrieve. I felt Russ's hand on my shoulder as the first pitch went out.

"Don't tell me the team's coach pitches to his own team at this age." It wasn't really a question. Russ saw the familiar figure tossing the ball from the mound. "What have I gotten myself into? T-ball has to be easier."

My giggle escaped. "Organizing the younger kids is more like herding cats. The kids run everywhere but to the right base. I thought you played Little League."

"Thirty years ago. I've got some homework to do before next week's practice." I felt his pain.

Champ's pay-attention head-butt quieted us both. The first batter struck out but exited the batter's box to applause. The second batter swung at the first pitch. Strike one. On the second pitch, he hit the ball.

The sound of the bat and ball contact sent Champ to his

I'm-ready-runner-in-the-blocks pose. Waiting for the command.

The batter dropped the bat and ran toward first base. Anticipation vibrated through Champ's hind legs. "Champ. Hold." The ball rolled past the pitcher's mound. It was fair.

"Champ, bring it back," I yelled.

The bat dog took off like a sprinter. He ran across home plate, picked up the bat, and returned it to me. The stadium went wild, applauding and screaming his name. I had to love Champ's popularity and his work ethic. He performed flawlessly.

I felt bad for the batter who'd made it to second on an error. He'd done the heavy lifting. All Champ had done was retrieve a bat. Maybe Clark Sugarland's comment concerning a dog on the field affecting the batter's self-esteem had been justified.

Champ fetched bats for four long innings before we exited the field. Although Champ seemed ready to stay longer, I wasn't. I had too much to do. As with everything else to do with Champ, fans delayed our departure. Officer Casey Ann called out from behind the concession stand as we tried to leave.

I hardly recognized her out of uniform. Not because she wasn't competent, but I'd never known her no-nonsense bun hid long, flowing dark hair. "Let me get you both a cookie. They're from Nell. RJ has them sent over after every game. The kids love them."

Who didn't? I would've bet nothing could stop me from getting to Police Headquarters except Nell's monster cookies. I hesitated. I hadn't eaten anything since that power bar hours ago underground. Russ didn't argue. He knew better than to get between me and Nell's cookies.

"The cookies go down great with chocolate milk or a juice

box. I forgot to pick up the coffee. Gabby's bringing it over," Casey Ann added as she handed us both napkin-wrapped cookies.

I passed on both the milk and juice. Coffee, on the other hand, I would've swallowed black.

Russ broke off a chocolate-less cookie piece for Champ. I wasn't sharing. (Maybe I had more in common with Woof's Chihuahua than I'd originally thought.) "I hear you're our new assistant coach," Casey Ann said to Russ. "My son will appreciate your guidance."

I'd forgotten her son played baseball.

Russ nodded. "If I'd known about the cookies, I would've volunteered sooner."

Casey Ann smiled. "RJ is amazing. He single-handedly supplies the Barkview teams with equipment, uniforms, and gameday snacks. He really cares about this town and our kids. Makes my son's life richer."

"I didn't see RJ at the game," I said. "Does he usually come?"

"He does. He's not a cookie eater, though."

"Blasphemy." I savored the yummy peanut butter crunch. "How does he take his coffee?"

"Two blue sugars. No cream." Casey Ann patted her stomach. "Wish I didn't have a sweet tooth."

"You and me both." Didn't stop me from devouring the cookie, though.

We thanked Casey Ann and walked east on Oak Street past City Hall to Police Headquarters. We met the chief, Hunter, and Sandy in the chief's office. I didn't ask why Hunter had been included. Sandy sat in the hot seat, holding up well under Uncle G's direct questioning.

"I'll charge you with obstruction if you don't come clean."

The speed of his toothpick rotation indicated the degree of Uncle G's annoyance.

My mother-bear instincts kicked in and I jumped into the fray. "Hey. If you have a problem..."

Uncle G cut me off. "Russ, did you know Clark intended to close the baseball card museum?"

So, the chief had spoken to Amanda. "Clark says he hasn't decided," I interjected quickly. He hadn't actually said those exact words, but I could tell.

"He has. He arrived to preview the Candy Catcher card exhibit and discovered the card was missing. He gave Amanda thirty days to inventory the collection and tie up loose ends." Uncle G's booming voice left no doubt as to the truth. Even the dogs' ears twitched.

I'd failed. Amanda had to be devastated. Had my decision to protect Woof caused this? "But we know where the card is." The words slipped out before I could stop myself. Guilt did that to me.

Uncle G's toothpick paused mid-spin. "When did you intend to tell me that?"

Champ's exasperated exhale made me feel even worse. I couldn't give up Woof. Not yet. I was so close I could feel it. I tried changing the subject. "Closing the museum doesn't make sense. Clark told me if he could find the Owen baseball card that he'd bid on it. That doesn't sound like a man ready to shut down his family's museum." Unless Clark had played me. I'd bought the whole family expectations thing. He'd seemed so sincere.

"He urgently needs money," Hunter added. "Yesterday, he approached me to value the museum's collection."

Was the financial situation at Canine Caramel worse than Aunt Char thought?

"Was the Candy Catcher card part of the deal?" I asked.

"Yes. I asked about it. It's by far the most valuable item in the museum," Hunter added. "I questioned his ownership. He insisted he could persuade his niece to sell it."

"That will never happen," I muttered. All this drama. Maybe Woof had been right to protect the card.

"Clark seemed certain he'd have his niece's agreement," Hunter replied.

Had to wonder how Clark had known that. Unless he had something on Ella or someone she loved, I doubted she'd bend.

"Where is Clark?" Russ asked. "I want a word with him."

I agreed. A conversation was a necessary first step. "I'll talk to Amanda. Maybe we can fix this."

"I'll go too," Sandy added.

Uncle G's growl stopped me mid-stride. "I'd like to know who has the Candy Catcher card." The chief sat back in his desk chair. I wasn't escaping his Rock of Gibraltar determination. No one was going anywhere without providing that answer. I was on my own. Russ's look said he'd follow my lead.

I chewed my lip. I needed a delay tactic. "Owen's grandson." I didn't wait for a response but scooted out the door with Champ and Sandy on my heels.

CHAPTER 20

Sandy drove Champ and me to my Jag parked at the museum. The stadium lot was by no means full, but the tailgaters' tents reminded me game time loomed.

"Amanda can be volatile. She'll go nuts when you tell her you know where the card is but refuse to give her any details. I really should go in with you," Sandy said. "If only to direct fire."

"We're friends. I need to do this on my own." Responsibility stunk sometimes.

"If the perp who stole the card didn't break the glass case or plant Champ's necklace, who did?" Sandy asked. "And who has the remaining three cards?" She let that sink in before adding, "Amanda had access and is connected to Sully through her aunt's association with him. When she realized the card had been stolen, maybe she got mad and broke the case."

Sandy's reasoning had merit. I'd considered it. Amanda could be critical, but her moments generally spiked and cooled in no time. "There has to be more to it. I owe Amanda an apology at the very least for accusing her of being involved."

"Russ would disagree," Sandy replied knowingly.

I really hated it when she parroted my conscience. The guilt didn't sway me though. "I'm taking Champ with me."

"A genetic licker. That'll help." I heard Sandy's dry comment. I just didn't want to believe it. Sandy scratched his ear. "Sorry, boy. You're a lover, not a fighter." Champ's goofy tongue half-hanging out of his mouth proved it.

"Don't underestimate him. He saved us from suffocating. He led Russ and Hunter to the secret room."

"Don't give him qualities he doesn't have," Sandy warned.

I scratched Champ's ear. "Don't listen to her. I think you're Super Dog." My child's voice even surprised me.

Sandy parked by the blue awning next to Amanda's SUV. "I'll be out here waiting. I'm not leaving until you come out."

Let's hope it wasn't in a body bag. Despite my bravado, my knees still shook as I entered the museum.

Amanda air-hugged me in the lobby. I swear the Candy Catcher bronze's critical eye stared right through me.

"You heard what happened? Clark closed the museum. I told you he was gunning for me," Amanda announced.

"I'm sorry, Amanda."

Guilt must've been written all over my face because Amanda's eyes lit up. "You found the Candy Catcher card, didn't you? I knew you would." She took a deep breath, her relief real. "I can fix this. I'll call Clark right now. Tell him it was just a prank." She rattled on, moving like a busy bee hopping topics as if they were fragrant flowers. "You cut this one close. The game starts in a couple of hours, and I need to reset the exhibit."

The wait for a pause took forever. I finally interrupted. "I don't have the baseball card."

She went from all smiles to shock. "What? Then why are

you here? You still have a few hours. You can't give up." She gulped, emotion overwhelming her.

"I know where the card is."

"You do?" She'd said it as if she didn't believe me. "Where is it?"

"There's a problem," I replied.

"What's the problem? Get it." Her fiery demand had to be stress talking. "We don't have time for complications. The Candy Catcher card goes on display in less than four hours."

"It's not that easy. What if I tell you I located the Owen card too."

Amanda's wide-eyed pleasure kind of made it worthwhile. "I'm overwhelmed, of course. I never expected that. Will they sell us the card? Clark will have to get the money."

"The owner is willing to loan it to the museum, but..."

"But what?" I flinched under her sharp, penetrating gaze.

"They want to know the identity of the owner of the remaining three Fab Five cards."

Amanda bit her lip. "I-I don't know. Let me talk to the owner. I can convince them that the card belongs here."

If sheer will could sway, she'd win. "The name or nothing. It's a deal breaker." I repeated Woof's demand, half-expecting a challenge.

Amanda answered, "I was one of the bidders. On behalf of the museum," she added quickly. "I know Austin Bruns bid."

"He's made no secret of that," I agreed.

Amanda's brows knitted. "I don't know anyone else. RJ would be the only person who might know, and I doubt he'd tell." I believed her. I'd deduced the same thing.

"I'll call him." Amanda drew her cell phone from her pocket at gunfighter speed.

My headshake stopped her from dialing. "The curious

thing is that you didn't ask why the Owen card's owner wants the information."

"I, uh..." Amanda refused to meet my gaze. "I'm just excited for the baseball card's return."

I noted her weak response. "Your aunt was Sully's assistant. You know about the secret room." I laid out my concerns, hoping she would deny it all.

She didn't. "Everyone knows about the secret room. It's an urban legend." Amanda jerked her fingers through her pixie-cut hair.

"But you know how to open it."

No denial. That bad feeling played havoc with my stomach. "Did Sully mistreat your aunt?"

"What? No. My aunt was good friends with Sully's wife. They made her costumes together."

"Then why hide it?" I asked.

"I didn't. Grandma K knew. I told her when she recruited me to run the museum. She chuckled. Said I had character and told me I'd fit right in."

That sounded like Grandma K.

"Why does any of this matter? My aunt passed away a long time ago."

I needed answers, not a brush-off. "What matters is who you told about the secret room."

"Everyone. I talk about it on the museum tour."

Either she was a great actress, or she really didn't know what I was talking about. "When did you find the secret room?" I quit asking easy questions.

Amanda looked ready to bolt. No doubt about it. She'd found the room. "Two years ago. A field mouse scared the crap out of me when I was waiting for the elevator. I tracked it down the next morning and found the bat rack. I knew the room had to be near there."

"Because Sully was an Illusionist?"

"Partly. My aunt taught me some tricks. She told me a lot about Sully."

"Like what?"

"The key would be a baseball bat. My aunt told me every doorknob and rail in his home was shaped like a baseball bat. Drove Sully nuts that he only had daughters."

"All successful doctors. You'd think he'd be proud."

"You know how jocks are. Wait. How do you know?" Realization struck. This wasn't a social visit. "What's going on, Cat? How did you find the secret room?"

"Sheer luck." And Sandy's diligent research, but Amanda didn't need to know that. "Why didn't you tell anyone you found it?"

Her sheepishness surprised me. "I kept it as a kind of Hail Mary with Clark. He's been threatening to shut the museum down for years now."

"What did he say when you told him about it?" I asked.

"I didn't. He was in a mood. Not listening to reason. I didn't think the time was right," she explained.

Her logic made some sense. "You know the Fab Five the best. Would Austin Bruns have a reason to want to get even with the Sugarlands?" I asked.

Amanda shook her head. "As far as I know, Karl remained friends with his second baseman until the man's death. You're thinking about the crime scene, aren't you?"

I nodded. "I felt the perpetrator's anger."

"I don't understand the question. You already know who stole the Candy Catcher baseball card," Amanda said.

"The person who has the card didn't destroy the exhibit."

"So, what you're saying is two people tried to steal it? That's crazy," Amanda said.

Verbalized, it sounded too ridiculous to be believed.

171

Amanda continued, "Whatever you think about Austin, he's a big advocate of bat dogs in the major leagues. He'd never allow Champ's name to be associated with controversy."

She was right. Champ's necklace at the crime scene had to mean something else.

"Is there anyone else who knows about the secret room?" I asked.

"Not that I know of. Clark needs the baseball card. He's run Canine Caramel into the ground, and his dear aunt left the most profitable part of the family's holdings to his young niece and put your aunt in charge of her interests."

That could make anyone mad and desperate. Why incriminate Champ? And how had Clark gotten the dog's necklace?

"Do the Fab five baseball cards really tell their batting secrets?" I asked.

"I've been told. I looked at the Candy Catcher card. There are only a few lines that looked like an afterthought drawn into the design."

"And..."

"I have no idea what they mean or if they mean anything. If it's true, the information would be priceless."

No kidding. It would offer a reprieve to a man on the brink of financial ruin.

"Did RJ authenticate the Candy Catcher's bat?" I asked suddenly.

I saw Amanda's confusion in her knit brow. "There was no need. Karl donated it himself. It was the first piece in our collection. RJ studied it a couple of years ago. He asked if we had issues with ants. Ants? Like I'd not have a decent pest control company."

Did RJ doubt the authenticity of the Candy Catcher's bat? Offering him a private showing of the real bat just might be the leverage I needed to entice him to disclose the anonymous baseball card buyer's identity.

CHAPTER 21

If appealing to RJ's love of baseball failed to get him to identify the anonymous baseball card buyer, bribery would have to do.

I waved to Sandy pacing in the parking lot, waiting for me as promised. I expected relief, not concern. She'd found something relevant. Her squinty eye tell never lied.

Her words gushed out. "RJ's import company supplied Canine Caramel with the faulty packaging that's caused the company's downward financial spiral."

Not necessarily criminal.

"He also organized that timely tour when Ella witnessed the break-in," Sandy added.

"Why? What link does he have to Clark Sugarland?" I asked. Without motive, I had nothing on the man.

Sandy shook her head. "I'll keep digging. Has Russ gotten anywhere following the money trail? I think he needs to look at RJ."

That twinge in my stomach agreed. I reached for my phone. Back pocket empty? I patted my jacket. No phone.

"I must've left my phone in the museum." Where else

could it be? I handed Champ's leash to Sandy. "I'll be right back." I retraced my steps to the door I'd just exited and pulled the baseball bat–shaped door handle. My nail cracked when the door refused to budge. I tried again. Locked? Amanda had been here a few minutes ago. Something wasn't adding up.

"Stay here with Champ. I'm going inside through the tunnel."

"What's going on?" Sandy asked, alert.

"I don't know. It could be nothing," I said.

"It isn't," Sandy replied.

She'd verbalized my fears. "I think Amanda's going to run."

"Why? You mean she wrecked the Candy Catcher display? I'd have bet money on Clark."

"Amanda gave me this odd look when I asked if the Candy Catcher bat in the display had been authenticated. I think she realized that I knew about the hidden bats."

"You think she will steal the original Fab Five bats?"

"I hope not. If the investigative team left a ladder behind I can check if the bats are still there. If not, I'll go into the museum through the secret room. Stay here and stop her from driving away until I return," I said.

"No problem." Sandy's confidence came with a vision of four flat tires. "Aren't you even a little nervous about going down into the secret room again?"

"More like desperate." I reached into my glove box and removed a six-inch, weapon-quality flashlight. I took a deep breath as I closed the car door and brandished the flashlight like the club it was. Over my shoulder, I said, "Watch your back."

I arrived at the players' entrance a few minutes later. The white-haired guard, dressed in a Candy Catcher jersey and pants with a Barkview centennial logo, greeted me with a smile. "Where's the bat dog?"

"He's coming. Mind if I go up to the suite and prepare?" I managed a sincere smile.

The man looked over my shoulder. "Sure. Anyone who's a friend of Champ's is a friend of mine."

Champ duty did have its perks. "Busy day?" I asked.

"Yeah. The police left about an hour ago. Can't have them scaring the kiddos. Can you believe it? The secret underground room exists." The guard pressed his forefinger to his lips. "Shhh. It's a secret."

Any wonder how the Barkview gossips got their information? I nodded. No one needed to know Sandy and I had been locked inside.

I waited for a distraction, then slipped under the Do Not Cross Police Line tape into the stairwell. Thanks to Russ, the entrance was open. I switched on my flashlight and peered into the inky darkness. No shadows. Nothing moving. Was I too late? Or had I been wrong? I hoped for the latter.

I balanced the flashlight barrel beneath my armpit and started down the expandable ladder, my light bouncing off the rock walls as I descended. At the bottom, I shone my light on the wall harboring the bat cabinet. For a second, everything looked the same. Relief surged. I'd been wrong. I savored that feeling for a moment before I saw the ladder leading into the museum hanging down the wall. Someone had dropped it from the museum. I checked the cabinet. Empty. Amanda had taken the bats.

My chance to catch her ticking away, I struggled to climb the unsteady rope ladder. At the top, I pushed on the trapdoor. It didn't budge.

If Amanda had barricaded it, I'd never get it open. If I exited the way I'd come in, Sandy would be engaged long before I arrived.

Before I could decide my next move, providence intervened, and the museum hatch slid open.

"Do join us, Cat." Any hope that Clark or Austin or even RJ was involved vanished the moment I heard the familiar, unbending voice. Amanda stood above me, though I hardly recognized her steely gaze.

It was only twelve feet down. I could jump back down into the secret room, away from danger, and let Sandy stop her outside.

"I wouldn't if you want to see Sandy again." Sandy appeared in my line of sight, her wrists bound in front of her in a glob of blue painter's tape. No decision to be made. My pulse pounded in triple time as I climbed the ladder in slow motion.

I entered the museum directly behind the five wax figures, dressed in their game-day attire, who had a secret worth killing for. On the floor lay five deeply-grained bats with caramel-stained knobs and handles, each signed with a flourish.

"Where's Champ?" I asked.

"He took off after a rabbit," Sandy replied. "That dog never listens."

Champ followed directions perfectly. Sandy had sent him for help. I needed to buy time. "How did...?"

"I saw you leave and snuck up on Sandy," Amanda said.

Sandy's nod agreed.

"So, this was always about the Owen card," I said suddenly, too angry to be afraid of the handgun aimed at my heart. A precise calmness—the kind where nothing ruffled me—settled over me. Russ called it survival mode. I'd fallen for Amanda's lies. "The Owen baseball card was going to be on loan to the museum. Why didn't you just wait for it to arrive?"

Dust coated Amanda's pixie-cut hair and jersey. "Hands in front of you."

I obeyed. I had no other choice. With the gun leveled on me, Amanda ordered Sandy to wrap the blue tape multiple times around my wrists. No easy task when her own hands were bound, but she did it loosely. When the time presented itself, she'd given me a chance to escape.

"I never wanted it to end this way. I couldn't take the chance that you knew where the bats were. Without them, the baseball cards are worthless," Amanda explained.

Not exactly worthless. She'd known the moment I asked about the authenticity of the Candy Catcher's bat. "You are the anonymous buyer. The Fab Five cards were bought and paid for by embezzling from the museum. That's why Clark wants to shut it down."

Her snarl shocked me. "You think you're so smart, Cat. I don't have the three baseball cards."

She hadn't denied the embezzling.

Amanda continued, "But I know who does, and he wants the Fab Five brought down as badly as I do."

I'd been right. "Why? What did Karl Sugarland do to you?"

"Karl? Nothing. Sully killed my mother," Amanda insisted.

"Your mother died in a DUI car accident." Sandy's monotone forced both of us to listen carefully to hear her comment.

Amanda ignored that truth. "My mother and aunt were identical twins. That's how Sully's tricks worked."

"So, the assistants didn't just vanish and appear? What happened?" I asked softly, dialing down Amanda's anger my first priority.

"Sully killed my mother and staged it to look like a car accident." Amanda's remembered pain was real. She believed every word she'd said.

I had to keep her talking. The longer we delayed, the better Russ's chance of finding us. "What happened?"

"They were working on a disappearing and reappearing bit that required my mom to float from the ceiling. Something went wrong, and the line broke. Her neck snapped."

I gasped. "You saw it?"

Amanda nodded.

This vendetta started to make sense. "That's traumatic. It was an accident. Why didn't they report it?"

"It wasn't an accident," she screamed. At that moment I saw her insanity.

More quietly, she added, "My mom was afraid of heights. She'd downed a few vodka shots."

I saw where this was going. "How many shots?"

"Enough for her to think she could fly."

Witnessed by her young daughter too. "It was a terrible accident." I'm not sure I believed it, though. Why would a mother drink before performing a dangerous stunt? It made no sense.

"Sully knew she didn't want to do it. He threatened to replace her and my aunt if she refused. He gave my mom his booze that night for courage."

I felt her childhood pain.

"He murdered my mother then fired my aunt right after the funeral because she couldn't do his tricks alone," Amanda explained.

Not sure how that would play out in court, but it wasn't particularly chivalrous, but not illegal. "You want revenge. I get it. What do you want to prove?"

"Reveal Sully for the cheater he was," she replied. "He fixed the bats. Every one of the Fab Five's bats were modified."

"How do you know this?" I asked.

"Sully drank and talked. The baseball cards will tell me how to prove it. I just need the Owen card."

"It won't bring your mom back." Sandy stated the obvious. "And it will destroy a bunch of kids' dreams."

Not to mention shake the foundation of baseball, if somehow the Fab Five had cheated to improve their batting averages. I shared a glance with Sandy. We were running out of time.

Amanda caught our exchange and leveled her handgun at Sandy. "Killing you both has possibilities."

"It means you'll never know who has the Owen card," I said. "I am willing to trade if you tell me who bought the Sully, Wilcox, and Bertie cards."

Her evil laugh sent a chill through me. "So you can get them yourself and bury the truth? You'd do it for Barkview. Barkview always comes first." She spat her last words.

"My family comes first," I replied. But in a way she was right about Barkview. I'd kept many of her secrets and would likely keep more.

"That's good to know." Amanda toyed with a lock of Sandy's blonde hair.

I shivered, suddenly terrified. I couldn't believe it had come to this. Amanda had completely duped me. Her caring and dedication to all things baseball had only been an act. She'd been like a sleeper cell. For ten years she'd kept up the pretenses. Did that warm woman I thought I knew ever exist? "Take me instead."

"I'll not face your husband. There are some things worse than death. Sandy will die and you will know that you killed her for a"—she paused—"baseball card."

That statement struck me in the gut. No contest. Sandy was invaluable!

"My patience is running out, Cat. Tell me the owner's name now!" The gun shook in Amanda's hands. Her threats were real. To save Sandy, I needed to give up Woof.

"I'm done waiting," Amanda said.

"I understand you were mad that someone beat you to the Candy Catcher baseball card and wrecked the display case, but why did you stage Champ's necklace there?" I asked.

Her cackle sent a shiver down my spine. "Dogs don't belong in baseball. Henry thought..."

"Ella's father?" I asked.

"Who else? He believed every team needed a bat dog. He planned to move the museum to the Canine Caramel retail space and convert this museum into a bat dog training school."

"And you couldn't let that happen. You'd lose access to the secret room and the bats." I filled in the details for her. "Champ's popularity has given the bat dog committee new energy. But there are no plans for a bat dog training center. I don't think they'd even thought of it." The dots weren't connecting yet. There had to be more.

"Henry left notes for his daughter. He said she'd find them when she was ready."

"It was you Ella saw in the stairwell." Broad-shouldered and stocky: the description fit. "You were going to Henry's old office to destroy his notes."

It all made sense now. A traumatized child had grown into an angry, vindictive woman. Aunt Char would say Amanda needed help. A 9 mm pointed at Sandy and me messed with my opinion. I'd prefer locking her up and throwing away the key. "You're wrong about the bat dogs. They are special animals."

I didn't know what else to say. Time was running out. I needed a miracle.

It came in a flash of black fur magically flying across the hall. Champ retrieved the Candy Catcher bat and barreled into Amanda, leveling her with a single swing. It's true. Life's scariest moments happen in slow motion. The gun went off, a bullet whizzing by my ear, ricocheting off the Candy Catcher's bronze mask, and going who knew where while the museum shook as if it had been hit with a flash-bang explosion.

Champ's yelp terrified me. Had he been hit? Or Sandy? They both lay on the floor on top of Amanda. Champ's guttural growl sounded so Rottweiler-like I wondered if the black Lab had somehow transformed.

I must've nicked the tape on my wrists when I hit the floor, because the tape tore easily. I picked up the gun and leveled it on Amanda as Russ, Hunter, and Uncle G stormed in.

Situation neutralized, Russ took the gun out of my hands and pulled me into his embrace. "Are you all right?"

I nodded my head. Hunter tore the tape off Sandy's wrists and hugged her. She would be fine—better than fine. "Champ?"

"He's unhurt." I felt the Lab's cool nose against my hand. I knelt to scratch him. He licked my face. I didn't even pull back. Not that I'd admit that. The dog had saved my life and Sandy's.

"Champ broke through the doggie door as we arrived."

"His timing was perfect," I said. Still too close for comfort, but... "I don't know where the bullet went."

"I do." Uncle G held up two halves of the Candy Catcher's bat. Nestled in the wood were two iron fishing weights. The added mass would have affected the swing.

"Let me see!" Cuffed, it still took two officers to hold Amanda back. "Something is inside the bat. I knew it. Sully was a cheat and a liar. Everyone must know."

Uncle G seemed to consider her statement. "What I see is a bullet lodged inside signed wall decorations coated in caramel. Apropos for Canine Caramel's lobby bat display."

"No! I don't believe it." Her shriek hurt my ears. "The Fab Five were..."

"Talented boys." Uncle G waved to the officer to take her away.

A simple answer for a complex question. Had the Fab Five really cheated? All the players had passed away. No one could confirm which bat had been used in play and which had been decorative only.

Sandy, with Hunter's arm around her, huddled around the damaged bat. Right now, Sandy fascinated him more than any batting secret.

My heart warmed for them. I was getting used to this. "Wait a minute. Amanda. I will tell the Fab Five's story. You have my word."

"A watered down Barkview version," she spat.

Likely. "It's the best you'll get. Who has the baseball cards?"

I guess she believed me. Restrained on both sides, she could only nod. "Like the bats, Karl wanted the cards kept in the family."

"Clark has them," Uncle G said with finality. "Take her away."

But did he? The caramel told another story.

CHAPTER 22

The national anthem played in the background when I sought out RJ in his press box, which was overflowing with baseball enthusiasts dressed in their favorite team's attire. I understood how successful RJ's marketing techniques were. Normally, I wouldn't interrupt, but I had less than three hours to find the three remaining baseball cards to restore the Candy Catcher card to the display.

"I'd appreciate a minute." I didn't give him an option. I turned tail and left, giving him no choice but to follow or appear rude. RJ was never impolite.

"What can I do for you?" His once-over found me wanting. I didn't care. I'd tried to run a brush through my worse-for-wear hair, but the overall effect hadn't improved much. I still looked like something the cat dragged in. Fortunately, my husband loved me exactly the way I was.

I motioned for RJ's silence as applause rocked the stadium. They'd introduced Champ. His mom, Melissa, worked on the field with him tonight. I didn't miss the spotlight, except for the parking privileges. The dog's joy at being on the field chasing bats and spreading his doggie cheer had touched me.

Overall, I enjoyed my time with the black Lab. He was a mellow, happy dog with the heart of a lion. He didn't bark much and loved to be with his humans no matter where they took us. Russ had issues with his shedding, and his table manners needed work. Having to protect my food from my dog would not be sustainable.

"I've located the original Owen baseball card. The owner is willing to loan it indefinitely to the museum if you are willing to do the same." I went out on a limb with that truth, but desperation did affect my negotiation skills. His little start made it worth it. I was on the right track.

"I also have the original Fab Five bats. Four of them are in perfect condition." The fifth had given up its secret to save both Sandy and me. I'd never regret that. "I know the secret, and I think you do too." The metal weights had been engineered specifically for each player's strengths. Talk about ahead of their time. Nothing was illegal about it then, but it was just not sporting. It could never happen today, which likely meant the Fab Five's batting records would stand for a long time.

No hiding his reaction to that truth. "Why do you think I care?"

"Because you're a Sugarland," I replied.

"Now, Cat."

"When you refused the caramel at the hospital, I wondered. When I learned you don't eat Nell's cookies and only use artificial sweeteners in your coffee, I knew for sure. The Sugarlands are all diabetics."

"A lot of people have diabetes," RJ said.

"Only half a percent of people are Type I diabetics."

He didn't deny anything.

"I don't blame you for wanting revenge against the Sugarlands. A son of the great Candy Catcher deserves to take his place in Barkview, and you have. You did it on your own merits. You're a self-made man and should be proud of your accomplishments. I bet you could run Canine Caramel more efficiently. Before you destroy the family business, please think about Barkview and what the institution means to this town."

RJ smiled. "Your aunt is a great lady who has chosen well in you. You will carry on the tradition woven into this town's fabric. I pray I will do the same someday."

His compliment touched me. I'd always considered myself lucky to be in Barkview, not the other way around.

"I am not trying to destroy Canine Caramel. I've already issued a credit for the faulty packaging," RJ said.

"His mistake or yours?" I asked, but I knew.

"It has been rectified. And that is all I will say about it," RJ replied. "I have been searching for the Owen card for a long time. I am pleased it has been found. I will also loan my three cards to the museum with a security clause."

I chuckled. I couldn't help myself. "The museum is looking for a new director. I suggest you consider accepting the position, at least as an acquisitions adviser."

"I would propose a joint venture if Canine Caramel is amenable."

My turn to smile. "I think your brother will be pleased to meet you."

"I know Clark Sugarland."

"True, but he does not know you. The question is, why is it a secret? Your mother was legally married to Karl."

"And divorced. I didn't know about Karl until my mother passed in 2012. My mother dreamed of being a Hollywood star. She married Karl to get out of Iowa and divorced him as soon as she reached Hollywood. She married a caterer whose fried chicken reminded her of home. She raised six children, who gave her fifteen grandchildren and seven great-grandchildren. She achieved her stardom in every school play and puppet show she produced. I'm not looking for a family, Cat. I'm building a legacy."

Canine Caramel had found its CFO, though that might take some convincing of both men. I didn't need a legal document or a hand on a Bible. RJ Ruff would live up to his commitments. I extended my hand. "That, RJ, is what Barkview is all about."

CHAPTER 23

Under Russ's watchful eye, the Candy Catcher baseball card was viewed by all who made the trip to the museum after the baseball game. Clark, RJ, and Woof ruled the event, promising that more cards in the series would be on display shortly. Viewing the five cards together would happen at a later date, but we already knew the secret. How we'd all missed the family resemblance between Clark and RJ shocked us all. Together, they would do good things.

Historic as that was, the game had proved to be the same. One of the Barkers' hitters batted .524. He didn't break the Candy Catcher's best game average, but he did get a nod to the major leagues. Which I'm guessing he preferred.

Sandy and Hunter huddled together near the Fab Five exhibit, seeing only each other. Was he the one for Sandy? Time would tell. New love was a great thing to be enjoyed. For now, the future could wait. They'd figure it out when they needed to.

While Barkview celebrated, unanswered questions still bothered me. Much as I wanted to know what really happened the night of the Canine Caramel fire, I doubted I would ever have the answer.

I convinced the coach to contact Ella's mom and insist that he needed his batting statistician. I know Ella enjoyed the game from the coach's box. I found her afterward in the museum, smiling as she watched the crowd.

"You did the right thing donating the baseball card," I said.

"I know. It was worth it, you know." Her seriousness reminded me of Grandma K.

"What was?" I asked.

"If I'd sold the card, I could've gotten away from here." She gestured toward her rambunctious little brother, terrorizing anyone he could—"right now. I'll survive three more years until I go away to college. Then, I'm out of here."

Any doubt Ella Sugarland was an amazing young woman vanished. I wonder if I'd have been so circumspect at her age. "No doubt you will. Want to go on a little adventure?"

Her eyes lit up. "Sure. Where are we going?"

"To find something that may change your mind about leaving Barkview."

"Not a chance."

At least I had her attention. "Come on." We exited the museum and walked around the stadium to the players' entrance. "We'll need your access card."

Ella scanned her card. "That's why you invited me. Isn't it?"

I only smiled. She didn't need to know about the connecting tunnel today. Someday, yes. Today was about her legacy.

We rode the elevator to the second floor and exited. People still milled on the sofas in the VIP area, but for the most part, no one paid attention to us as we strolled down the hall to the general manager's office.

She stopped me from entering. "We can't go in there. It's a private office."

"It's okay. We have permission." I did. I'd already asked the GM if I could take some pictures of the Sugarland desk. He assumed I wanted them for a story. I didn't correct him.

Ella frowned but relented. I turned on the lights as we entered. The office was a shrine to Barkers baseball, with historic stadium photos interspersed with ball player awards mounted on the eggshell-painted walls. That Ella didn't give the baseball greatness a second look, instead focusing on the large double desk dominating the floor space, confirmed my suspicion. She'd been in here before.

"This was your Nana Dolce's desk. It's similar to the White House *Resolute* desk. It was commissioned..." I trailed off, hoping she'd fill in the rest. Ella did.

"From the wood on the ship Nana Dolce sailed to America in." Ella's fingertips ran the length of the desktop. "My father told me about it."

I'd thought so. "He showed you where the secret compartments are, too, didn't he?"

"N-no." The nice thing about youth is an untrained ability to lie.

"Ella, I'm a reporter—a living lie detector. Sure you want to test me?"

She gulped. "It's just full of family stuff."

She'd read it. "Your family is entitled to secrets. We all have them. I just need to know who set the Canine Caramel fire in 1952." If I interpreted her gape correctly, my directness stunned her.

"Ella." My warning tone worked.

"I don't know, and that's the truth. Grandpa Karl denied it."

My intuition just about sang. "Your Nana Dolce was the caramel maker. Wasn't she from France?"

Ella's dark hair bounced as she nodded. "She was a war bride. She came to America in 1919."

The pieces fit. The Candy Catcher had had other dreams for his life. Nana Dolce and Grandma K had built and preserved this candy empire for a hundred years. With Aunt Char's guidance, Ella would get her chance someday.

Ella disappeared behind the desk. I heard the click of a door opening and the sound of rustling papers and relatching. When she stood, she rested her hand on a worn leather journal as if it were a Bible. "The fire was an accident. Nana Dolce had found a Roman caramel recipe. She left the experimental caramel in a slow boiler and went home to serve her husband dinner. He was a stickler about eating precisely at five. Would have driven me crazy."

"Me too." Russ had his quirks. Fortunately, inflexibility wasn't one of them.

Ella continued. "She intended to return afterward to complete the recipe. The Fab Five..."

"All five of the players?" I asked.

She nodded. "...entered the factory to do their ritual bat dip into the caramel before the next day's game. The rest was bad luck."

For a lot of people. "Did Karl ever know the truth about the fire?"

"Yes. He blamed himself anyway. Guilt brought him back to Barkview."

"But love kept him here," I said. "Love for your father and uncle. And this amazing baseball team that he built." I meant every word. "Like the Candy Catcher, your father had a dream, too. I think that's why Champ intrigues you so much. You think bat dogs should be on both the minor and major league rosters."

Ella's smile agreed. "You're a good reporter."

"That will never change," I replied. "Following your dreams isn't a single path. Sometimes it's a winding road." Who knew what that road would be for Ella, but she was off to an excellent start, with the possibilities only limited by her choices.

For a minute, I doubted she understood my message, but then she smiled. "I get it. It's like storming the castle. There's more than one way to save the princess."

Philosophy interpreted in Gen Z terms. I guess I could communicate with kids.

The End

I hope you enjoyed your adventure in the dog-friendliest place in America. To learn more about Barkview and Cat's next adventure, visit www.cbwilsonauthor.com.

Sign up for *The Bark View*, a monthly update on all things Barkview, including

- *Friday Funnies*: pet-related cartoons
- *WOW!* A dog did that?
- Recipes from *Bichon Bisquets Barkery's* canine kitchen
- Cool merchandise ideas from the *Bow Wow Boutique*
- Not to mention Barkview news and fun contests.

Don't miss Cat's next adventure when Cat goes to Hawaii in *Puppied to Death*.

COMING SOON: PUPPIED TO DEATH

A murder, an ancient rivalry, and a puppy you can't help but love...

A frantic plea from her sister sends Cat Hawl on a rescue mission to Hawaii. What should've been simple mediation between Lani and their mother turns deadly. Not only is a tea sommelier murdered, but a puppy has turned the crime scene into a dog's breakfast, and Cat's trouble-prone sister is nowhere to be found. Has the killer taken Lani, or is she on the run?

Since local law enforcement suspects the worst, it's up to Cat to dig deeper. With her mother and the Miss Marple Mahjong Mamas' help, Cat uncovers an ancient rivalry rooted in the Forbidden City. Can a thousand-year-old tea reading be the cause of the current puppy pandemonium and mounting body count?

Join Cat as she follows the tea leaves on a chaotic journey anyone who has ever raised a puppy will relate to.

About the Author

The award-winning author of eight Cozy Pet Mysteries and counting, C.B. Wilson's love of writing was spurred by an early childhood encounter with a Nancy Drew book where she precociously wrote what she felt was a better ending. After studying at the Gemology Institute of America, she developed a passion for researching lost, stolen and missing diamonds—the big kind. Her fascination with dogs and their passionate owners inspired Barkview, California, the dog friendliest city in America.

    C.B. lives in Peoria, AZ with her husband. She is an avid pickleball player who enjoys traveling to play tournaments. She admits to chocoholic tendencies and laughing out loud at dog comics.

To connect with C.B Wilson:
www.cbwilsonauthor.com
www.facebook.com/cbwilsonauthor

ACKNOWLEDGMENTS

To my writing cheerleaders, Pam Wright, Dee Kaler, Becky Witters, and Brandi Wilson, who endlessly listen to my ideas, edit my spelling and grammar, and help research and test recipes: I couldn't do it without you.

For research and police procedure assistance, thank you to Sargent Jeff Daukas with the Glendale, Arizona, Police Department. I assure you any errors are entirely my fault.

Many wags to Michael and Melissa O'Donnell, who allowed me into Champ's amazing world and inspired me to believe a dog belongs alongside Cooperstown Greats. I will forever be grateful to Mike and Valerie Brest for initiating it.

As always, Melissa Martin. You keep me sane.

Made in United States
Cleveland, OH
24 November 2024

10860535R00127